W9-BUE-244

The Callahan Cousins

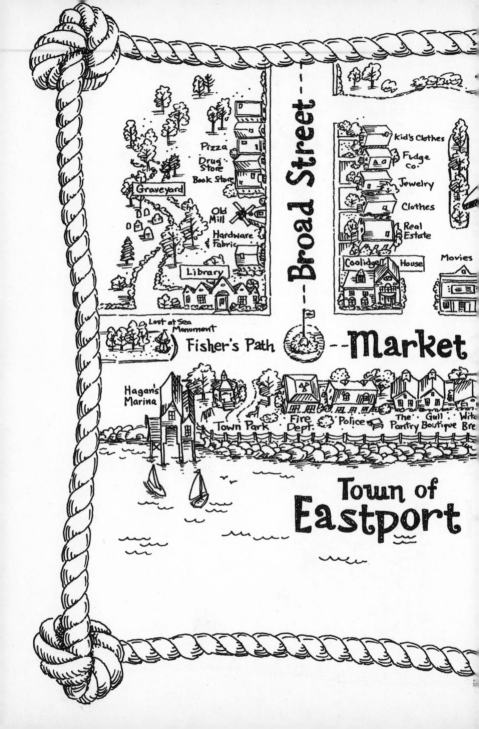

The *Callahan Cousins*

Home Sweet Home

by **Elizabeth Doyle Carey**

LITTLE, BROWN AND COMPANY
New York ❧ Boston

Copyright © 2005 by Elizabeth Doyle Carey

All rights reserved.

Little, Brown and Company

Time Warner Book Group
1271 Avenue of the Americas, New York, NY 10020
Visit our Web site at www.lb-kids.com

First Edition: September 2005

The characters and events portrayed in this book are fictitious.
Any similarity to real persons, living or dead, is coincidental
and not intended by the author.

Library of Congress Cataloging-in-Publication Data

Carey, Elizabeth Doyle.
Home sweet home / by Elizabeth Doyle Carey. — 1st ed.
p. cm. — (The Callahan cousins)
Summary: As their summer on Gull Island continues, the four twelve-year-old
Callahan girls busy themselves with redecorating the Dorm, dealing with their
mean neighbor Sloan, and uncovering a secret about their family's past.
ISBN 0-316-73692-9
[1. Interior decoration — Fiction. 2. Secrets — Fiction. 3. Cousins — Fiction.
4. Grandmothers — Fiction. 5. Islands — Fiction. 6. New England — Fiction.]
I. Title. II. Series: Carey, Elizabeth Doyle. Callahan cousins.
PZ7.C2123Ho 2005
[Fic] — dc22   2005002299

10   9   8   7   6   5   4   3   2   1

Q-MT

Printed in the United States of America

Book design by Alyssa Morris

The text was set in Mrs. Eaves and the display was set in Bickley Script

For Alex, Liam, and Finn, with buckets of love, and for Liam and Finn's cousins: Julia, Caroline, Holly, Lucy, Penny, James, Peter, Bosco, Iñigo, Alvaro, Hugo, Santi, Stoddy, Austin, Frick, Olivia, and Angus.

Cousins forever!

"Send them to me," said grandma Gee.

And so they did.

⌐⊙

CHAPTER ONE
The Dorm

$\mathcal{N}$eeve Callahan stood with her hands on her hips, drew herself up to her full height (which was more elfin than impressive), and surveyed the room before her. She took in every detail of the neglected space — grimy windowpanes, bare wooden walls that were exposed down to the studs and beams, beat-up old furniture, and the stench of mildew — and was instantly against the idea of moving in. She closed her bright blue eyes, sighed in exasperation, and ran her fingers through her spiky black hair.

"What a dump!" she declared finally, her tiny, freckled nose wrinkling in distaste.

"You sound just like Bette Davis in *Beyond the Forest*," said her cousin Phoebe, without even lifting her eyes from the thick, boring-looking book she was reading. Phoebe's long limbs were folded into a pretzel and her white-blond hair was piled on top of her head and skewered with a pencil to hold it in place.

"Oh, whatever, smarty-pants," growled Neeve affectionately. Even though they were complete opposites — Phoebe was a cautious bookworm and Neeve a bouncy social butterfly — Neeve was amused by Phoebe and her seriousness, and, deep down, very impressed by Phoebe's wealth of knowledge.

"Come on, Neeve! It's not *that* bad," interjected Neeve's other cousin Hillary. Neeve watched as Hillary flipped one strawberry blond braid over her shoulder, then briskly squatted to pinch a bug between her fingers and flick it out the open door of the Dorm. Neeve grinned with pride at brave, outdoorsy Hillary, their very own Denver-bred cowgirl. Bugs didn't particularly bother Neeve, either — because of her dad's foreign service job she'd lived all over the world in places where bugs were just a daily fact of life — but she stole a glance at her squeamish cousin Kate to see if Kate had noticed. Although a bug problem would surely deter Kate's moving plans, Neeve couldn't bear a shrieking Kate right now.

Luckily Kate was wandering around, engrossed in her inspection of their potential new living quarters. Her round blue eyes were so busy drinking in every detail that she hadn't even noticed the rather large cobweb that clung to her glossy brown hair.

"So, Kate, it's a disaster, right?" prodded Neeve hopefully. "Not even worth redoing?"

"Hmmm? What? Oh, but *yes*! It *is* worth it! Definitely!"

said Kate. Her usual enthusiasm bubbled to the surface as she emerged from her redecorating trance, eyes twinkling and cheeks dimpling in happiness.

Neeve scowled, irritated at herself for even asking for a status report; she'd known perfectly well that she wouldn't get a straight answer from Kate, so why had she even bothered to ask? Ever since their grandmother Gee had told them the night before that they'd earned the privilege of redecorating and moving into the loft-like Dorm at the foot of her property, Kate had been poring over her stash of design magazines, making lists and doing idea sketches with her colored pencils, and just itching to get in here and experiment with her decorating schemes.

Neeve had to admit that it *was* a privilege to be offered the Dorm. The Sound, Gee's rambling twelve-acre property at the tip of Gull Island's summer resort area, was gorgeous, and studded with magical places: the Promised Land cove, the Fallen Down Trees, the huge garage, the bathing pavilion, the boat shed. But the Dorm was the coolest. White-shingled and black-shuttered, just like the main house, it was nestled behind a tall privet hedge that provided privacy and a sense of independence to the Dorm's inhabitants. There was a deep tunnel through the hedge, with a little white picket gate in it that you had to go through to enter the Dorm's tiny private yard. It was sort of like going through the back of the wardrobe to Narnia in *The Lion, the Witch and the Wardrobe*.

The Dorm had originally been a stable, but Gee, along with

Neeve's grandfather Pops, had converted it years ago to serve as a low-maintenance guesthouse for the many visiting friends of their nine children. However, it had retained its quirky lay-out and now gave off the air of a playhouse of sorts or a fairy-tale cottage; it was a place for young people to be independent of adults while still safely nearby.

But even though the Dorm was usually reserved as guest quarters for visiting teenagers (so it was a huge honor that Gee had said the four twelve-year-old cousins could move down there for the remainder of their summer visit), and even though Gee had told the girls they were welcome to redo it any way they liked, Neeve still wasn't sold on it. She and her cousins already had really cute rooms, right across the hall from each other, up in the big main house, and Neeve was happy there. Plus, to be totally honest, she'd had it with moving.

Because her mom was from Ireland and her dad was a diplomat, Neeve and her younger brother and sister had moved all over the world: from Dublin to Karen, Kenya, then Shanghai, China, and now Singapore. Everywhere they went, Neeve had to make all new friends, learn a whole new lan-guage, find her way around a whole new city, and try and make a homey space for herself in whatever new house they had. Now, all Neeve really wanted in life was a home base; a place she could always escape to, that would be forever unchanged. Her room in the main house already felt that way, and it killed her to move again.

Yet one glance at the other three cousins and she knew she

was done for. Kate was thrilled by anything that required artistic or homemaking talents, both of which she had oodles of. Hillary was excited by a new challenge, especially one that involved planning, goals, and hard physical labor. And Phoebe liked the fantasy aspect of it all — the Dorm reminded her of all the books she'd read about boarding school antics and orphans and things like that; she was looking forward to living out those no-grown-ups-around kind of adventures.

Neeve was sunk. They were moving. She blew her short black bangs up off her forehead in frustration, and considered her options. For one, she could make a stink so that no one could move; but then everyone would be mad at her and she'd have no one to talk to all day. Anyway, she hated crybabies; her dad's motto was even *Callahans don't cry.*

Neeve's second option was to let the other three move down here while she stayed in the main house by herself. But the solo life was not for Neeve. She'd just get lonelier and lonelier. So her only choice was number three: to move down here with the others.

If you can't beat 'em, join 'em, Neeve decided, for the millionth time in her life. She was nothing if not adaptable; and, truth be told, she *was* good at moving. She heaved one last self-indulgent sigh, and employed her no-fail emergency coping strategy: she slapped a big smile on her face and faked the enthusiasm until it became real.

"So what are you thinking?" she asked Kate.

"Well . . . ," Kate began, spinning in a circle as she surveyed the big downstairs room. "Besides the basic clean-up . . . The couch and armchairs need new slipcovers . . ." And Kate was off and running, ticking ideas off on each of her fingers.

"Hey guys, let's check out the upstairs," interrupted Hillary, ever the explorer. She grabbed hold of the fixed ladder that led to the sleeping loft above and nimbly scampered up it. "Ooh!" she called from upstairs, her voice echoing out across the rafters of the living room. "I haven't been up here in years! Come on!"

Neeve was hot on her heels, never one to be left out, but a reluctant Phoebe and tentative Kate trailed along behind them.

"Let's go, sissies!" called Neeve. The other two weren't as brave as Hillary or as bold as Neeve, and they usually had to be coaxed into situations that might cause risk to life or limb. Neeve did rather enjoy being their drill sergeant.

She reached the sleeping loft and instantly sneezed from the dust. It was hot up there — the windows hadn't been opened in ages and the heat of the midsummer afternoon was trapped under the roof. She looked around. Neatly aligned along the wall to her left were four white iron beds, their ticking-striped mattresses stripped of linens. Each bed had a small white bedside table with a little lamp on it, and opposite the foot of each bed, along the railing that overlooked the living room, was a white wooden dresser. One end of the loft had a tiny bathroom and an even tinier closet, and the other end had a door that opened out onto the back of the Dorm, where there was a sleeping porch and a ladder up to the little look-out tower thingy on the roof.

Hmm, she thought. *It would be fun to share a room with everyone all together.* She and Kate currently shared a room, since they'd been the first to arrive, but deep down, Neeve knew she'd have more fun rooming with Hillary or even Phoebe. *Maybe the Dorm would be more fun than the big house!*

After their Dorm explorations, the girls retreated to the pool up at the main house. Kate rustled up a snack for everyone: seven-layer Mexican dip with tortilla chips, warmed-up Parmesan puffs, and other leftovers cooked by Gee's Irish housekeeper Sheila for a party the night before. Phoebe darted upstairs to grab their notebook (the cousins used the notebook to keep track of various summer projects and adventures). And now everyone was relaxing on the fluffy pink-and-white-cushioned lounge chairs and discussing their redecorating plans. Just above them, running along the rear of the enormous white-shingled house, was a sun-splashed brick terrace, where white iron patio furniture was topped with the same slightly faded pink-and-white-flowered cushions; huge round planters full of pale pink geraniums attractively echoed the fabric's pattern. And sprinkled along the tree-ringed perimeter of the back lawn were a slightly overgrown grass tennis court, a trim little herb garden, a trampoline, and a little fingernail of a beach, with a dock and a peak-roofed bathing pavilion. Down to the left, behind the hedge, was the Dorm, the current topic of conversation.

"Okay, so what's our plan?" Phoebe asked the group as she moved ahead to a new section of the notebook and neatly titled it "The Dorm."

Kate listed the things she wanted to get: high-gloss white paint for the walls, floors, chests, tables, and lamps; white canvas for slipcovers and curtains; cute fabric for throw pillows; and some burlap or grass-cloth to glue on the coffee table to refinish it.

But now that Neeve was in on the plan, she wanted to put her two cents in, too. The one thing she'd always insisted upon with all of her family's moves was total control when it came to the decorating of her own space. She'd been able to sort of compromise with Kate in their room here in the big house because it was basically already decorated. But if Kate had her way with the Dorm, it wouldn't feel like home to Neeve at all. She knew she had to step in now, before Kate got too out of hand, so she wracked her brain for fun ideas.

"Hey, uh . . . my old school in Africa had an entire wall in the corridor painted with blackboard paint. It worked just like a regular blackboard, and you could leave messages for your friends between classes and stuff. It was really cool. We should do that."

"Yeah!" agreed Hillary.

Phoebe nodded and added "Blackboard paint" to the list.

"But where?" asked Kate. Neeve could tell that Kate's finely honed sense of propriety was offended by the thought of a big black wall in her otherwise white-based color scheme.

"Well, maybe on the wall where the ladder is? Or even a big square of it, like in a painted frame on the wall?" suggested Neeve.

Kate nodded. "Yes. A small frame would be good."

Small. *Humph!* thought Neeve. *We'll just see about that.*

The talk went on with Neeve suggesting outlandish things — like gluing sequins all over the bathroom mirror frame for a "bling" effect or ordering cheap Chinese slippers over the Internet and then gluing them around the ceiling as a border — and Kate trying to tone her down. But, of course, Hillary and then Phoebe supported Neeve; and Kate, who was the one who would actually know how to make these things happen, started to fume. She sat on her lounge chair, twisting her long, dark hair into a bun and then crossing her arms in a huff.

Hillary seemed honestly perplexed by Kate's behavior. What Neeve loved about Hillary was that she was not a girly girl. Hillary didn't play mind games or have big mood swings, and she wasn't much good at indulging other girls' little dramas. It made her very relaxing to be around.

"Katie, are you mad about something?" asked Hillary kindly.

"No," said Kate, looking off into the distance. "Well, maybe."

"What? What is it?" pushed Hillary, truly curious.

"Well, it's just . . ." Kate sniffed and her eyes welled up with tears. "*I'm* supposed to be the crafts one, and the decorating one. And now Neeve has all these fun ideas and you guys are all into her stuff and no one wants to do what I want to do." She quickly wiped at her eyes and stared off at the water, half-embarrassed and half-relieved by her revelation.

"Oh, for goodness' sake!" said Neeve in an impatient but not unkind tone. Sometimes she went too far with bossing Kate around, and then she always regretted it; Kate really was sweet and sensitive and Neeve could forget that when she was annoyed with her. But Kate could just be so babyish! Neeve rose from her lounge chair and went to sit next to Kate. "We can do your stuff! I don't care. Really! I was just trying to think up some fun things — like stuff that would be as fun to *do* as it would be to *look at* after it's done. But we don't *have* to do it."

"But your ideas are actually a lot better than mine," Kate persisted.

Neeve bit her lip thoughtfully. She really wanted the Dorm to be *her* way — she hated to live in a place that wasn't her style — but she'd just have to be patient for now until she could get Kate to come around. "Look, why don't you figure out how to get the basics in good shape. The walls, the floors, and the furniture. Then, if we all agree that we should jazz everything up, we can do that after, alright?"

Kate looked down. "Okay."

"Katie . . . ," singsonged Hillary. "Is it really okay? 'Cause we're not mind readers . . ."

Kate smiled and looked up. "Yeah. It's okay. We could do that."

"Grand," declared Neeve with a relieved sigh. Whenever Neeve's emotions ran high, her Irish accent and her use of Irish words increased. After all, she'd lived there for the first eight years of her life. "What do you say to a rummage through the attic?" Neeve proposed as a change of scenery. Kate loved the attic.

Re-energized by their snack and eager to clear the air from the fight, everyone agreed, and they headed up to the third floor of Gee's house.

▲

"It's boiling up here!" cried Hillary, who hated being trapped indoors.

"We don't have to stay long," said Kate comfortingly. She was back to her usual motherly self now that she felt secure again. "We really just need to look around with an eye towards stuff we could use down in the Dorm. Like a stack of old suitcases might make a neat side table in the living room, or something."

Phoebe had gravitated back to the old piles of *Life* magazine that had interested her on previous visits, and Neeve was poking around in the corner, looking at old beach umbrellas that were stored there. Meanwhile, Hillary had spied a big box labeled "Family Photographs," and Neeve watched as she crossed the attic to check it out. Neeve knew that ever since May, when Hillary's parents had finalized their plan to get divorced and her dad had moved out, Hillary had been worried about being cut off from the Callahan side of the family (not that that would *ever* happen, but Neeve could see why she worried about it, anyway). Consequently, Hillary was magnetically drawn to old photos and family stories and stuff like that; it was as if she needed physical proof of her position in the family.

Hillary opened the box and called "Jackpot! Look at all this stuff! We could do a whole family gallery out there, just like Gee has in the back hall." Gee's classically decorated house had fourteen bedrooms and lots of halls, which meant lots of wall space. Gee had been filling the empty space for years with a chronological exhibit of their family photos.

Neeve abandoned her umbrella search and went to look at Hillary's find. There were stacks of framed photos and Hillary was pulling them out one by one, without even really looking at them. It seemed she just wanted to get a sense of how many were in there. Neeve paused to study a picture of her grandfather, Pops, looking dashing in his Navy uniform. Even though he'd died when she was two, Neeve was glad she'd had the chance to know him.

There were some really funny old photos of Gee, and then some of the girls' four dads with their other brother and their four sisters, all lined up as if for a Christmas photo. Neeve spied another photo of her dad, peeking out from under a pile near Hillary. She reached to pull it out and a couple of other pictures slid to the floor with a clatter.

Hillary jumped.

"Sorry," said Neeve, distractedly glancing down at the 5-by-7-inch photo in her hands.

And then the world stopped.

The photo was of Neeve's father, very young and very dressed up, with a woman in a wedding dress. They were holding hands and cutting a wedding cake together, and people in the background were toasting them with raised champagne glasses.

But the woman was *not* Neeve's mother.

Neeve gasped.

"What?!" demanded Hillary, startled by Neeve's outburst.

Neeve looked up quickly, as if from a dream. "What?" she asked in a panicky voice.

"Are you okay?" Hillary looked at her with concern.

Neeve flattened the photo against her chest. Hillary obviously hadn't looked at it when she'd removed it from the box. Neeve was speechless — a very rare occurrence.

"Uh . . . um . . . Yeah. I'm fine. Just grand." But her mind was swirling and she felt like she might be about to pass out. "I think the heat is . . . really getting to me," she added in a stroke of genius.

"Then let's get you some fresh air!" said Hillary, all too happy to escort out of the attic. "Guys!" she called to Phoebe and Kate. "We're outta here. Neeve's passing out on me. We need fresh air. You can stay if you want, or we can all do it another day."

Hillary quickly escorted Neeve downstairs and out to the

terrace off the elegant pale blue living room. While she went to get Neeve something to drink, Neeve thought quickly and dashed inside to hide the photo of her dad in a random drawer of a spindly-legged antique side table. No one would ever find it. She was sure of that. Now she just had to figure out if there was anything *else* she was sure of in her life.

CHAPTER TWO

The Invitation

*H*illary returned with a tall glass of ice water, into which she'd thoughtfully inserted a few slices of lemon left over from the party the night before. Neeve accepted it gratefully, had a long sip, and then rested her head back against the cool fabric of the chair cushion. She rolled the frosty glass along her forehead and closed her eyes. She couldn't even think straight; questions kept ricocheting around her brain and the image she'd seen was seared into her eyes, even when she closed them. *Why was her dad in a wedding picture with a stranger?*

Hillary looked concerned. "Are you sure you're okay? You might have heatstroke or something. One of the girls on my track team had it in the spring." She paused. "Do you want me to go get Gee or Sheila?"

"No!" Neeve's eyes snapped open. She hadn't meant to answer so forcefully, and she smiled at Hillary's slightly shocked expression. "Sorry. I just mean, don't bother them. I'm grand. Really." She straightened up in her seat and placed the glass on the table beside her. The last thing she needed was Gee sympathetically taking her hand and offering her a cool compress. Neeve knew she'd break down and spill the beans to Gee before she'd even had a chance to think through what she'd seen.

Kate and Phoebe tumbled out the French doors from the living room with worried expressions on their faces. Kate rushed to her side. "Gosh, Neeve. You look really pale. Are you okay?"

Neeve smiled grimly. "I'm fine. Just overdid it a little, I think."

"Maybe you should go lie down or something," suggested Phoebe helplessly, her eyebrows knitted together in concern. Phoebe wasn't the most demonstrative person in the world; it could take a while to even figure out if she liked someone at all, so Neeve knew that Phoebe was really worried when she showed any kind of emotion. Neeve felt grateful for all the sympathy and attention, but right now, she knew she needed to be alone to think things over. She rose unsteadily to her feet.

"I think you're right, Bee. I'm just going to go upstairs for a little bit and put my toes up, as my other grandmother says." She smiled again wanly and went inside, leaving the other three on the porch to discuss and worry about her.

"We'll come check on you in a little while . . . ," called Kate. As she wandered through the rambling house and up the grand staircase, Neeve felt a flash of guilt for all the mean thoughts she'd had about Kate. Kate really could be so sweet.

Upstairs, in the large room she shared with Kate, Neeve lay down on her bed, not even bothering to pull back the wildly colored batik bedspread she'd brought from home. She wished she'd grabbed the picture from the drawer downstairs so she could study it, but at the same time, she never wanted to see it again. She closed her eyes against the late afternoon sunlight that slanted into the room through the big multipaned windows, and took a deep whiff of the floral-scented potpourri she kept on her bedside table. Its aroma always helped her to clear her mind when she needed to think.

Her dad was the eldest of the Callahan brothers, the second child of the nine. He *had* been a little bit on the old side when he'd married her mum; thirty-three to be exact. It was *possible* that he'd been married before. Possible logistically, that is, but not emotionally. How could he ever have picked someone besides her mum? They were made for each other. A sudden thought occurred to her and her stomach dropped. *Oh my God!* she thought. *What if he has other kids?!*

Hot tears began to squeeze out of her eyes, and Neeve brushed them away impatiently. She hated crybabies and complainers. She twisted and turned on her bed for a while, and then fell into a fitful sleep. The shock had worn her out. When she awoke, the sun was beginning its orangey-yellow descent into the sound and there was a light tapping sound on her door.

"Come in," she croaked.

Gee opened the door and entered the room, coming swiftly and gracefully to perch on the side of Neeve's bed. Tall and elegant in her butter-yellow sweater set and crisp white linen pants, Gee looked as beautiful as ever. Her snow-white hair was artfully tousled (It was plain to see whom Neeve had inherited her cowlicks from) and her pink lipstick was in place as usual, but her bright blue eyes betrayed her worry.

"Sweetheart! We've been so worried! I came in to check on you a little while ago and you were out cold! I didn't want to wake you then because you looked like you needed the rest, but if you hadn't stirred this time, I was going to call over to the clinic."

"Thanks. I'm okay, though," said Neeve. She managed a sleepy smile and rolled onto her side. Gee reached to smooth back Neeve's unruly bangs and gently feel her forehead. Her hand was cool and soothing and made Neeve have to close her eyes again.

"It must have been the heat and the excitement of the weekend," Gee continued. "The girls said you went from the closed-up Dorm to the attic and you just overheated. You were probably exhausted from the last few days, too." She patted Neeve's cheek gently, and Neeve opened her eyes again.

The weekend *had* been chaotic, Neeve admitted to herself, even though it had also been a blast. They'd spent all day Friday tearing around the sound in a boat while they tried to win a family feud against their enemy, Sloan Bicket. Then Friday night, much of the extended Callahan family — including their parents, a bunch of aunts and uncles, and about half of their twenty-two cousins — had arrived for their annual weekend visit, and there'd been a huge family beach picnic Saturday night. But everyone — including their parents — had left this afternoon. Even though she was a social creature by nature, Neeve had to admit she'd been exhausted even before she'd seen the photo in the attic.

But the nap had done her some good; she wasn't as shocked as she'd been before. Now she just felt deeply agitated by her need for more information, and she couldn't think of how to ask Gee. She also dreaded what she might find out. Whatever it was, it would change her life as she knew it. And she'd been through enough changes; she'd come to Gull and Gee's house to get away from all that. This was supposed to be her one true home — the one place in the world that was constant! Now, with the whole moving-into-the-Dorm thing and the photo of her dad, she felt betrayed by The Sound, as if she'd been lulled into a false sense of security and then had the rug pulled out from under her, in the place where she'd least expected it.

Well, she'd just have to be more vigilant, she decided, her usual spirit rising up to take over the lily-livered wimp that threatened to emerge from deep down inside her. Neeve Callahan wasn't a sissy! She could face up to any changes or curveballs that life threw her.

She sat up and energetically swung her legs over to the floor. Oops. She did still feel a little woozy. Gee stared at her with an eagle eye. Neeve knew Gee had learned a thing or two after raising nine kids, and she was also a very sympathetic person — the kind of person that strangers told their life stories to in line at the grocery store. Neeve had to put on a better show than this or Gee would make her stay in her bed for days! She'd wind up telling Gee everything just to save herself from dying of boredom in bed.

"You stay right here, young lady," said Gee, drawing Kate's pink mohair throw blanket up over Neeve. "I'm going down to the kitchen to get you a little cocoa and some cinnamon toast. If you feel better after that, maybe you should take a shower and come down to dinner. Or I could have Sheila bring it up to you. Let's just see. Now, back in bed and stay put!" Neeve meekly did as she was told and got back in bed as Gee left the room, her step strong and purposeful on the floorboards in the hall. Then she pushed Kate's blanket back off. It made her itchy.

Neeve sighed. Her dad had been telling her just yesterday (*Yesterday? Could that have been just yesterday?* Neeve thought distractedly. *It seemed like a million years ago*) how she was just like his mother, and Neeve guessed it was true. She and Gee were both strong and willful and a tiny bit bossy, but Gee was just a little more graceful about it.

Just then, there were whispers outside the door and the three cousins burst in.

"Are you better? We were so worried! Oh my God! You were passed out. Kate got Gee!" They were all talking one over the other and Neeve laughed, thankful for their energy and the distraction of them all.

"Quiet, savages! Don't you know this is a sickroom?!" She threw her pillow at them then, and they laughed, too.

"Oh, goody. You're better!" cried Kate, crossing the room to sit on her own bed. "Tell her!" she said, turning to Hillary.

"Tell me what?" demanded Neeve, sitting up against her headboard and drawing her knees to her chest.

The others were silent for a moment, but laughter was welling up inside them and their eyes shone.

"You'll never guess who called us while you were asleep . . . ," began Hillary teasingly. She plopped down in the cushy armchair by the window, and folded her legs up underneath her; she clearly meant to draw out the suspense.

"Who?" Neeve hated delays and surprises. She needed to know *now*!

"Sloan!" whispered Phoebe dramatically, her eyes wide as she perched at the end of Neeve's bed.

"No way!" yelped Neeve. "What did *she* want?"

Sloan Bicket was their enemy. Or she had been. Now Neeve wasn't so sure. Sloan was the meanest girl on the island — the same age as the four Callahan cousins, snotty, bratty, beautiful, and a year-rounder, meaning Gull Island was her full-time home. Their dads had all been summer friends on the island when they were growing up, but a running joke had turned into a family feud, and they'd had a major falling out. Hillary had recently made peace between the two families, laying the feud to rest, and now it seemed like Sloan wanted to be their friend.

"Get this," said Hillary drily, "she's having a sleepover party and she wants us to come."

"What?! Get out of here! You can't be serious!" Neeve was shocked for the second time that day. Would wonders never cease? "When?"

"This weekend." Hillary grinned.

"But we're obviously not going," said Kate.

"Why not?" chirped Neeve. "I say we go!" She loved making new friends and felt a special relish in turning former enemies into friends. Making friends was like a game, and she was really good at it.

"Come on, Neeve, you can't be serious!" said Phoebe. "She's evil! She probably wants us to come over so she can soak our hands in warm water after we fall asleep, and then she and all her giggly minions can have a laugh at our expense!"

"What's a minion?" asked Kate.

"Like a crony. A little assistant who laughs at her jokes and does her bidding."

Hillary laughed and shook her head. "I think most of the other girls seem kind of scared of her."

"Exactly," said Phoebe wisely, nodding her head.

"Oh," said Hillary. Neeve knew Hillary wasn't involved in the cliquey girl groups at her school, so she was sometimes a little clueless. Poor Hillary, so innocent. Neeve smiled her most persuasive smile at her.

"Well I think we should go. It will be an adventure! And anyway, we can check out her room and see if we can steal any cool decorating ideas for the Dorm." Neeve had already made up her mind; now she just needed to convince the others. She looked at Kate for her reaction.

"Oh no! No way!" said Kate. "You guys aren't roping me into this one. Uh-uh!" She shook her head emphatically.

Neeve turned to look at Phoebe. "Bee? Don't you want to, um, check out Sloan's book collection?"

Phoebe drew herself up to her full height, which was considerable, and stiffened her spine. She sniffed and said, "Puh-leeze. You can't sell me on that! Anyway, it's probably all Sweet Valley High and Olsen Twins books, with some witchcraft and voodoo books thrown in for good measure!"

Laughing, Neeve turned to Hillary. "Hills, I know you're in. I don't even need to ask you. Right?"

But Neeve could see Hillary wasn't so sure. Even though Hillary had kind of made up with the Bickets on the Callahans' behalf, Neeve knew Hillary wasn't crazy about Sloan.

Neeve let out a dramatic sigh. She'd have to play her trump card. "Well, I can see none of you is really interested in my complete recovery. If you were, you'd be doing anything to make me happy right now."

The others shrieked and then grabbed her, tickling her mercilessly, knowing how much she hated it.

"Stop! Stop!" she gasped. "I'm dying! I can't breathe!"

Just then, Gee arrived with her tray of snacks for Neeve. "Girls!" she reprimanded. "What are you doing to my patient?!"

"She's faking!" yelled Hillary. "She's fine!"

And she was, physically anyway. It was good to have these cousins for friends, Neeve thought, as Gee bossed them off her bed and out of the room. At least *they* never changed. She could always trust them to be true to her, no matter where she moved or how many new friends she had to make and languages she had to learn. The cloud that had been hovering just out of sight descended upon her again as she thought of her dad in that shocking photograph. She almost asked Gee point-blank, and then she chickened out. What if she didn't like what she heard?

But she resolved to persuade the cousins to go to the sleepover. She needed the distraction of an invigorating social life, especially if it involved a challenge. Neeve could be very convincing when she wanted to; she knew she'd get them to come around. It would take her full attention, though, and that would be a good thing.

CHAPTER THREE

Ditch 'Em!

On Monday morning, the girls awoke early to get to sailing clinic on time. Neeve, who tended to be theatrical in her clothing choices, dressed for power. She needed to feel strong and in control to deal with the images of her dad that hovered in her mind and to convince the others to attend Sloan's sleepover. Therefore, she was wearing her superhero outfit: black Lycra bike shorts, a leopard print skin-tight tank top from Japan, and a fitted black, zip-front windbreaker with a collar that stood up on its own. She had slicked her hair back with gel for an aerodynamic look and then topped it all off with wraparound mirrored sunglasses and a tribal African choker that was supposedly made of bone (you could never be sure what the craft dealers were selling on the street in Nairobi. It could very well be plastic, but Neeve liked to go along with the bone idea, imagining it to be gazelle or some other fleet, exotic-but-not-endangered animal of the savanna). The total look made her feel invincible, like an avenger from a comic book.

Kate had done a double-take when Neeve got down to breakfast, and Neeve smiled, knowing her look was having the desired effect. She poured herself her usual mug of black coffee from the percolator by the huge cooking range, then crossed the room and slid into the green-upholstered banquette at the long farmhouse table with the others. Hillary had grinned and said "Sweet necklace," and Phoebe had just grunted. Phoebe was always cranky in the morning because she stayed up way too late reading in her bed every night.

After a delicious breakfast of Sheila's homemade corn muffins and strawberry jam, the girls wheeled their bikes to the end of Gee's crushed-seashell driveway to begin the two-mile ride to Hagan's Marina.

"Isn't Sloan going to want an answer today?" asked Neeve innocently when they reached the road. Each girl hopped onto her red bike. (After too many lost bikes over the years, Gee had finally spray-painted all of the bikes at The Sound entirely red; now everyone on the island knew whom the red bikes belonged to.)

"I guess," said Hillary. After they turned onto the paved Fisher's Path that would take them into town, she let go of her handlebars and folded her arms to ride no-hands.

"We all know what our answer is," said Phoebe.

"Yes?" said Neeve.

"No!" yelled Phoebe, and she rode hard to get ahead of

Neeve, signaling that the discussion was over. Meanwhile Kate, the least athletic of the cousins, dropped behind.

"Why do you want to do it?" Hillary asked Neeve, now that it was just the two of them.

"Because it will be interesting! And challenging! We could meet new people . . . have fun, everything!" As much as she hated moving and changing schools and stuff, Neeve really did love meeting new people. It was what always saved her. She found new people energizing. And, hey, if she was moving again — even if it was only from the main house to the Dorm — she might as well get some new friends out of the deal. That was the way it always went.

Hillary put her hands back on the handlebars of her bike and turned to look at Neeve. "Do you really want to do this?" she asked.

"Yes." Neeve smiled her most charming smile and fluttered her eyelashes persuasively.

Hillary paused to look over her shoulder at Kate, who was completely out of earshot. Then she looked at Phoebe, far up ahead. Finally, she said seriously, "Alright. I'll say yes and we can just convince the other two. And if we can't convince them, then they can just stay home."

"You rebel!" shrieked Neeve, lifting her hands off the handlebars to clap.

Hillary grinned.

Neeve pedaled happily the rest of the way to clinic, all the while thinking about what she should wear to Sloan's party.

Once inside the A-frame Hagan's Marina building, Hillary and Neeve let Phoebe and Kate walk ahead to meet their cute teenage sailing instructor, Tucker. Then they quickly sidled over to where Sloan was standing with her little group of girls, all of whom looked up to her worshipfully.

"Hey, Sloan," said Neeve casually. *Was Sloan even tanner than last week? Was such a thing possible?* wondered Neeve as she stifled a giggle.

"Hello," said Sloan, looking Hillary and Neeve up and down. Neeve was glad she'd worn her warrior princess outfit today. She'd known that she'd need its power.

"We just stopped by to say thank you for inviting us over this weekend," Hillary began. "We're not quite sure . . ."

"We'd love to come!" interrupted Neeve.

Hillary gave her a dirty look and Neeve pretended she didn't see it. Hillary started again. "What I was going to say was, Kate and Phoebe aren't so sure about sleeping at someone's house who they don't really know, so . . ."

Sloan suddenly lunged forward and dragged the girls aside. Neeve was confused and she glanced at Hillary, who looked equally confused.

"Not everyone is invited," Sloan whispered through gritted teeth.

"Oh, right, sorry," said Hillary.

"Anyway, what Hillary's trying to tell you is that she and I would love to come, and we're just trying to convince Kate and Phoebe to come along, too. They're a tad bit shy, you see . . ." But Neeve faltered; she suddenly felt like she was betraying the others, talking about them like this with Sloan.

Sloan looked at Neeve levelly and said, "Then ditch them." Sloan's green eyes were clear and remorseless, and Neeve was suddenly taken aback. Was this some kind of a challenge? Even though Hillary and she had agreed on the same idea, it seemed like a much meaner and more disloyal thing to do when it came out of Sloan's mouth.

Neeve bristled. "We certainly will not ditch them! They're our cousins and we're a team!"

"Sorry," said Sloan, sounding anything but. "But they sound like losers. So if they're holding you back socially, then I say leave them behind. I couldn't care less if they come. Just let me know by Thursday, because I need to get organized." And with a flip of her long, silky brown hair, she left Hillary and Neeve and returned to her posse.

"On second thought . . . ," whispered Hillary.

Rage swelled in Neeve's chest like a balloon about to burst. She put her hands on her hips in her trademark feisty-girl position, and watched Sloan rejoin her eager little group of followers. "On second thought *nothing!* Now I want to go to the party just to get revenge!" spat Neeve. She looked out at the dock where Tucker and the rest of the beginners group was waiting for them. She saw Kate — shortish, a little chubby, but so cute — and Phoebe, all long, long legs and long white-blond hair she'd inherited from her Swedish mother — standing waiting for them, and she felt like the worst heel in the world. They were so innocent and loyal and she'd nearly sold them out! All for what? Making friends with a mean girl? Well! She'd never tell them what Sloan had said about them, but she did still think they should all go to the party. Only now it was to get even.

But first they needed a great plan.

Over deli sandwiches at Callie's Cupboard after clinic, Hillary and Neeve batted around revenge ideas. Phoebe finished her lunch quickly and sat with her arms folded across her Indian-print shirt; she was still refusing to attend the sleepover, but she was intrigued by Neeve's sudden change of tune about Sloan. Kate listened wide-eyed as Neeve and Hillary suggested and then rejected far-fetched ideas such as smuggling Nair hair remover into Sloan's shampoo bottle, and SPF 45 sunscreen into her moisturizer.

"I don't get it," said Kate finally, her eyebrows knit together in confusion. "One minute you want to make friends with Sloan, and the next minute you want to torture her. What's the deal?"

Neeve sighed heavily, as if Kate were the most clueless individual in the world. "Things change, Katie. They just do." She shook her head slowly from side to side for emphasis and thoughtfully took a bite of her sandwich.

"Oh Neeve, you think you're so mature!" said Phoebe, amused but annoyed. "Why don't we just tell Sloan no and be done with it?"

Neeve's eyes regained their usual mischievous sparkle. "Because that's so boring! She's really a jerk and I think we should make her pay. Just a little."

Hillary had been quiet for some time. Now she spoke up. "What if we tell her we're coming and then bag at the last minute?"

"Evil!" shrieked Neeve. "But I love it!"

Phoebe rolled her eyes and Hillary grinned in pride.

"Or, you know what would be even better? We could actually *go*, but then say we want to call Gee to come and get us because we don't want to sleep there." Neeve's mind could work in very devious ways sometimes.

"That's really mean!" sputtered Kate. "Why would you do something like that?"

Neeve glanced at Hillary and then decided to play her trump card. "Because Sloan is mean. She told us to ditch you and Phoebe and just come ourselves."

Kate gasped and Phoebe's jaw dropped open while her icy-blue eyes narrowed to slits. "What?!"

Hillary shook her head at Neeve. "Neeve, you shouldn't have said it."

Neeve folded her arms and smiled smugly. "But it's true." She knew everyone was on her side now.

"What a witch!" Phoebe said vehemently. "Fine. Count me

in, if only for revenge purposes." She huffed and folded her napkin into a perfect little square. "I feel like the Count of Monte Cristo!" she muttered.

Kate nervously bit her lip while she thought for a moment. She knew all eyes were on her. "Fine," she said, finally. "I'll go, too."

Chapter Four
Missing Persons

$\mathscr{B}$ack at The Sound that afternoon, Hillary made a quick call to the Bickets' to tell Sloan that they would all four come to the sleepover on Saturday. Afterward, Hillary reported to the others that Sloan had sounded so unexcited by their acceptance of the invitation that she wondered why they'd been invited at all.

"Who knows?" said Neeve. She was tired of talking about Sloan for the day. They had their plan for Saturday and now it was time to move on.

The day had become overcast, and a pillowy fog was rolling in off the water, so the plan was to work on the Dorm.

The girls had stopped at the hardware store after lunch to pick up some paint and other essentials for their redecorating project. As they pedaled up Fisher's Path and across the open causeway to North Wing, the northern end of the island where all of the summer people's large houses were, they passed Gee in her ancient Volvo station wagon.

"Yoo hoo!" Gee had called as she pulled the car over to the sandy strip between the road and the grass that ran alongside it. She leaned out her window and waved at the girls. "I'm on my way to a Ladies' Village Improvement Society meeting. Oh! Have you bought supplies for the Dorm?" When the girls replied in the affirmative, Gee called out the phrase that her children joked they'd put on her headstone one day: "I hope you charged it to me!" Gee had a horror of her children or grandchildren paying for anything that she could otherwise pay for. Her theory was that if you were with her, everything was on her tab, like it or lump it. She always said she'd rather spend her money (which was a considerable fortune) while she was alive than let the government take it in taxes after she died.

"Yes, Gee. Don't worry! You paid!" called Neeve.

"Good. Well, I can't wait to see what you do with the Dorm! Ta-ta! I'm off to my meeting! See you at dinner. Steak on the grill!" She pulled the car back onto the road and waved again, her fingers fluttering in the wind like a flag. Beyond her, the graying sound was getting choppy with little whitecaps from the increasing wind.

"Hey, you know what would be neat?" said Kate as they began pedaling again. "What if we do the Dorm redecoration as a surprise for Gee, and then we do a big 'reveal' at the end like they do on those TV shows?"

"Like, not let her see it while we're doing it, and then show her when it's all done?" asked Neeve. She didn't get a lot of their cable channels in Singapore, so she was forever trying to catch up on American television when she was on Gull.

"Yeah." Kate nodded her head, her face already red from the exertion of pedaling with three heavy paint cans in her bike basket.

"Okay," agreed Neeve.

"But let's not drag this thing out," said Phoebe sensibly. "The best part about those shows is they only have eight hours or so before the husband comes home from the football game, or whatever, so it's short. It's all about what they can accomplish in a really short span of time. They're very organized."

Neeve smiled. Leave it to neatnik Phoebe to appreciate the organizational details. "But it has to be cool," said Neeve emphatically. "I mean, there's no point in revealing something that's bland or boring or even *not ready,* just for the sake of impressing Gee."

"Well, in order to prove to Gee that we're mature enough to handle the responsibility she's given us," added Kate, "we'll need to keep to our word and finish it neatly and on time. We don't want to lose her trust now."

Neeve burst out laughing and swung her head to the side to look at Kate. "Are you for real?! Gee doesn't care if we do it at all! She just thought it would be fun for us!" Neeve's bike wobbled and she had to look back at the road ahead. "Where do you come up with this stuff? Responsibility. Maturity. Holy moly!"

Meanwhile, Kate had set her jaw and was looking defiantly ahead.

Hillary was standing on her bike pedals, trying to figure out how to do a wheelie. She sat down heavily, defeated by the weight of the ancient bike and the bulk of her supply-stuffed backpack. "Look, let's just make sure this doesn't turn into some summer-long, detailed project where we're trapped inside for weeks on end and never even get to sleep in the Dorm until our last night on the island."

"My point exactly," said Kate.

"Fine," agreed Neeve, shrugging theatrically. "Fine."

And so now they stood in the Dorm's entrance again, arms laden with cleaning and painting supplies. Everyone was looking to Kate for directions, and she was savoring the moment of being in charge.

"Okay," she said finally in a businesslike voice. "Phoebe and Hillary, why don't you do the upstairs? Sweep, then mop, then tape that blue tape around the edges like the guy at the hardware store said, so the paint doesn't go outside the lines. Neeve and I will clean and set up down here, then we'll paint. Bee, take the high-gloss paint for all that woodwork upstairs. I think that shine will look nice on all the beadboard and wainscoting."

"What the heck is she talking about?" whispered Hillary to Phoebe.

"Who knows?" Phoebe giggled and rolled her eyes. "Just do what she says."

Sweeping and mopping were chores that Neeve hated; Kate had probably assigned them to her just to drive her crazy, thought Neeve.

"Hey, you know what? I'm going to run up and grab that boom box out of the kitchen. We need some tunes in here while we're doing this." And before anyone could say anything, Neeve slipped out the door and ran through the gate in the hedge, then lightly up the small grassy hill, past the pool, and across the terrace to the back of the main house. She hesitated for a moment, since she knew she ought to walk in the kitchen door, but instead she quietly opened one of the French doors to the living room. With a quick glance around to make sure no one was there — not that anyone would be — she crossed the room in two quick strides and slid open the side table drawer where she'd hidden the picture of her father. She'd been craving another look at it.

Neeve gasped.

The drawer was empty!

She pulled the drawer out entirely and bent over to look in the empty hollow where it had been. No picture. Where could it have gone? She stood up, holding the empty drawer uselessly in her hand, and her gaze wandered around the room while her mind raced. Had one of the other girls found it? No. That was not possible. They would have mentioned it or acted weird or something. For sure. They hadn't even been in here in days, as far as she knew.

Gee? No. Gee was always so busy, she never had time to go looking in random drawers. She hardly even sat down, unless it was to return phone calls at her dressing table.

It could only have been Sheila, thought Neeve. She must have been cleaning in here and something made her open the drawer. She must have found the photo and put it away somewhere.

But where? Like a programmed robot, Neeve did a fast but methodical search of every other drawer in the room. Wrapping paper and ribbon in one. Place cards and note cards and a surplus of birthday cards in another. Coasters. Playing cards. Party favors and decorations. But no photo.

Darn it! Neeve sunk down heavily in one of the soft, overstuffed armchairs and rested her head on the fingertips of one hand. She needed to see that picture again. She had been ready for it this time. She figured that if she could just get used to the sight of the image, by repeated exposure to it, then she could summon up the courage to ask Gee, or maybe even — horror of horrors — her dad for more information about it. And now it was gone. So she couldn't examine it, she couldn't ask anyone if they'd seen it, and she couldn't discuss what she'd seen with Gee; she had just needed to hold it in her hands one more time to confirm that it was real.

A tiny part of her was even now starting to wonder if she'd just imagined it.

Neeve was in a kind of shock, but her well-honed survival instincts swiftly kicked in. Whenever she started to feel sad or hopeless — which happened often to a person who moved from country to country — she'd think of a quote her mother had once told her, from a play by the Irish writer Samuel Beckett. It had become kind of a mantra for her that she'd chant in her head when she was discouraged. It went: "I can't go on, I'll go on." Neeve knew that whenever the empty pit of sadness or loneliness threatened, she had to go on. There was no time for whinging (or *whining,* Neeve corrected herself; it was hard to remember to use the American words instead of the Irish words when she was here), because once that started, there might be no end.

For Neeve, the best way to avoid the sadness was to get herself with some other people ASAP. She always felt instantly better, even if it was just the *tiniest* bit better, when she wasn't alone.

So she took a deep breath, stood up, and trudged into the kitchen for the boom box. She could hear Sheila humming in the laundry room off the far end of the kitchen, but Neeve didn't call out a greeting. If Sheila had seen Neeve coming from the living room with an upset look on her face, she would've quickly put two and two together and there would have been a big to-do where it all came out, and Neeve definitely wasn't ready for that. This way, Neeve was able to duck in, snag the boom box, and sneak out, all without a conversation with Sheila.

On the way back down the hill, Neeve stopped in the thickened fog and stood stock still for a moment. She'd reached the midway point between the house and the Dorm, and both were so blanketed by fog that she couldn't make out either one. For a split second, she had the pleasant feeling that she was back in Ireland, where the summer fog rolled over the moors almost every afternoon in June and July. She could almost hear her mum calling her to come for a ride on one of the Connemara ponies, or her dad shouting for her to join him on a quick spin on the curragh. She took a deep breath. The fog also felt like Shanghai. On a rainy day, down by the docks, with the merchants singing out in Mandarin and some other weird dialect she didn't understand. The junks pulling up to the docks to disgorge their loads of fish. All at once, Neeve shuddered. Where was she? She could be anywhere right now. A panicky sense of dislocation started to overtake her, and she spun around, confused.

Neeve tried stomping her foot at herself. "*Stop this!*" she whispered. "*Get going!*" But she was rooted to the spot.

Then suddenly, "Neeve! Neeve! Where are you?"

Kate's voice was carrying through the fog, and the density of the air made it sound like she was right next to Neeve.

"Come on, you slacker!" Hillary chimed in.

Neeve was startled out of her paralysis, and with a nervous grin, she shook her head to clear it and headed back toward the Dorm. Of course she knew where she was. *I mean, duh!* she chided herself. But her knees still felt a little wobbly as she started back down the hill.

Back at the Dorm, Kate was finishing the floor cleaning and getting ready to coat the downstairs walls with paint. She was just dispatching Hillary to find a ladder up in the garage when Neeve returned. From the peeling sounds up in the loft, Neeve knew Phoebe was upstairs, still taping the floor. Neeve bent to plug in the box, and twirl the radio dial. They picked up all kinds of stations out here on the island — from mainland Rhode Island, of course, but also Connecticut, the Cape, and even Long Island — so there were lots of good music choices. Neeve finally settled on some reggae that would be acceptable to everyone, and went to grab a brush.

Kate glanced over at her and did a double-take. "Are you okay?" she asked. "You look kinda funny."

"Yeah. Just tired," said Neeve. She didn't need to dwell on her down mood. That wouldn't help it go away.

Kate narrowed her eyes and appraised Neeve. "Are you sure it's not that you're annoyed that I'm in charge? Be honest!"

Neeve smiled in true surprise. "No. Not at all! I swear. It's fun."

Kate looked at her a moment longer and then decided that she was satisfied that Neeve was telling the truth. "Okay. Then I'll just keep on bossing. I feel like you!" she giggled. "Why don't you do that wall?" Kate pointed across the room.

"Okay," said Neeve. Even though she was distracted by the

missing photo and her weird panic attack, being with the others quickly started to help, and the work of painting helped, too, of course. Listening to the music and the cousins' chatter, she went into a Zen-like trance and covered one wall and then the next, evenly and smoothly, in just under an hour. Even Kate was impressed.

By the time Sheila rang the dinner bell outside the kitchen door of the main house, they were halfway done with the painting. The girls cleaned up their stuff and neatly stowed it away. As they stood at the door to leave, Kate took a proud backward glance.

"It looks really good, you guys. I'm psyched!" she declared.

"Yeah, it's really . . . clean-looking. Like, fresh," said Hillary, groping for interior decorating vocabulary words.

"Hey, we didn't set a date for the reveal!" said Phoebe.

"Hmm . . . How about . . . next weekend? Like, a week from Sunday?" suggested Kate, mentally calculating the work they still had ahead of them.

"Okay." Hillary and Phoebe agreed and they made their way up the hill for dinner.

"Hmm." Neeve was noncommittal. She wanted to get past all the boring white-painting and get on with the real decorating. Her brain was bursting with ideas for little decorations in and around the Dorm, and she was frustrated with the pace of things. But at the same time, she couldn't see the point of rushing the job if the end product wasn't going to be fabulous. The Dorm was going to be their new home, after all!

They'd just have to wait and see where things were by next weekend, Neeve decided. If she could really get the others excited about her ideas and making the Dorm more the way she wanted it, then the deadline wouldn't even matter. She was sure of it.

CHAPTER FIVE

Drivers' Ed

$\mathcal{O}$vernight, the fog turned into rain, and the girls awoke to a heavy downpour that spattered the windows of the big house as if someone were throwing handfuls of water at them. When they realized sailing clinic would be canceled, Phoebe rolled over and went back to sleep, but the others got up for breakfast. Kate immediately started in on their "To Do" list of projects for the Dorm, trying to parcel out assignments. Neeve dreaded another day of boring old painting and wiping, so she told Kate she was taking the day off. Infuriated, Kate stormed upstairs to shower and dress, but she left them with a strong warning about their reveal date. Neeve rolled her eyes at Hillary and giggled, but Hillary just raised her eyebrows; she didn't want this to turn into a big fight, which is where things seemed to be headed between Neeve and Kate.

Gee returned from her early morning swim in the sound (every day, rain or shine!) and read the paper in her terry cloth robe, obituaries first, as usual. She listened as the girls suggested and rejected activities, occasionally lowering her reading glasses and interjecting ideas of her own.

"Why don't I take you girls down to the library with me when I go for my fund-raising meeting, and you could rent some films?" she'd say as she turned to a new section of the *Boston Globe.*

"Nah, that's too boring."

"How about a bake-off? Sheila could take you to the grocery store for ingredients and you could have a contest!"

"No . . ."

Kate came back as Neeve and Hillary were enjoying Gee's undivided attention, and she, too, quickly warmed to the game of rejecting Gee's ideas; after a while, everything Gee suggested cracked them up. But then she had an inspired idea that they couldn't reject, even for the fun of it.

"Why don't you work on some crafts this morning, maybe with some of those beads you bought? Or you could paint a bunch of those huge clamshells I've got lying around here someplace. I could use some new soap dishes. And I'll go to church and my library committee meeting, and then I'll come back here and . . ."

The girls were already shaking their heads when Gee dropped in this zinger: ". . . teach you to drive."

There was a silence, and then the three exploded. "Yes!"

"Do you really mean it?" asked Kate eagerly.

"I'm dying to learn!" said Hillary breathlessly.

Gee laughed. "Yes. I do think it's important that everyone know how to drive in case of an emergency. You could take turns going around the driveway." The Sound had a long driveway with a loop at one end. It would be an excellent place to learn.

"Done!" said Neeve. "Kate, get the beads. Gee, we'll be right here waiting for you when you get back."

Gee laughed again. "You might want to change out of your pajamas!" She stood to go upstairs for her shower.

The morning passed in a frenzy of beading: earrings, bracelets, a necklace, and even an anklet were completed before Gee returned at eleven-thirty. The girls managed to change into clothes, and Phoebe arrived somewhere along the way, rumpled, puffy-eyed, and mute: the usual morning Phoebe, just a few hours later than normal.

Neeve was drinking black coffee and Hillary was munching on a carrot stick she'd plucked from the ice-water-filled bowl of them that was always in Gee's fridge. A Diet Coke stood sweating on the counter in its can, ready for them to bring out to Gee as soon as she returned. After a brief stopping, the rain was coming down hard again, so they didn't hear Gee's car coming up the driveway.

The back door opened and Gee was there, giggling and shaking water off her umbrella, hanging her raincoat on the coat tree in the mudroom, stooping to ditch her rain clogs and place her purse on the bench.

"Well!" she declared. "We might want to wait a few minutes before we start, just to see if this rain tapers off."

The girls returned to their seats, momentarily disappointed. Gee took her Diet Coke and poured it into a glass and joined them at the kitchen table. She had a sort of old-fashioned policy that food containers of any sort were not allowed at the table: soda cans, ketchup bottles, mustard: everything had to be in a dish or a glass or it was bad manners.

"Nasty out there," she said, grinning like a little kid. Gee loved weather. Any kind, as long as it was extreme and dramatic. The girls nodded. "I saw Mrs. Bicket at my meeting this morning," she added, and suddenly everyone's attention was captured. "She said you girls are spending the night with Sloan this Saturday? Is that true?"

"Yup," said Neeve. She was the leader on this one, so she'd be the one to do the talking.

"Goodness, I thought you couldn't stand her!" said Gee in a whisper. Sheila was related to Sloan, and although Sheila had made it clear that Sloan was a brat and her family was completely unbearable, Gee didn't want Sheila to overhear her talking badly about the Bickets.

"Yeah," said Neeve. It was hard to explain, and actually, now that she looked at it from the cozy, happy haven of Gee's yellow kitchen, it did seem kind of mean of them to accept the invitation and then plot revenge. Neeve fumbled for an explanation, but it was Kate, of all people, who bailed her out.

"We just thought we should branch out a little. You know,

make an effort to get to know other people on Gull Island to make it a really complete experience here this summer." With her large blue eyes and rounded cheeks, Kate was the picture of innocence.

But still, Gee looked at her skeptically. "Okay. Well, then, we should make sure to buy a house present of some sort. Maybe pastries or something? There are an awful lot of you to impose on another family."

"It's a sleepover, Gee! Not a weekend visit!" protested Neeve, laughing.

"And anyway, we're not even going to really —" Kate stopped abruptly and all but clapped her hand over her mouth. This was the chink in the armor that Gee had been looking for. Her well-honed child-rearing instinct zeroed in on Kate, and the girls could practically see Gee's antennae rising.

"You're not going to what, my dear?" she asked in her sweetest voice.

"Nothing," said Kate guiltily. But the cat was out of the bag.

"Alright, everyone. Come clean!" ordered Gee. Her voice was still friendly, but they could tell she was serious.

There was a long pause, and finally Neeve said, "It was my idea. It's my fault."

The others chimed in, "No, it wasn't Neeve. It was all of us."

Neeve explained the situation to Gee, including the choice bits that Sloan had said about Kate and Phoebe. Gee listened quietly, taking in all the facts.

At the end, she said, "Well, I am proud of your loyalty to

one another. That's difficult to learn and once it's accomplished, it's a gift that will be with you all of your lives. However, I am distressed at the ill will that Sloan elicits from you all — though I do seem to remember her father and uncles having the same affect on your fathers — and I am let down by the way you've handled that ill will. Revenge is a terrible idea. It's a downward spiral that will suck you in, taking you lower and lower and draining all of your energy away from more productive endeavors. You need to move beyond that."

She looked around the table, catching everyone's eye to make sure they all knew that there were no innocent parties. Then she continued. "If you want to go to Sloan's party for the right reasons, for fun and to make friends, by all means, go and have fun. But if you are going there to get even with Sloan — or if you have no intention of actually staying — then I forbid you to go, only because you don't seem to be able to make that decision yourselves. Furthermore, if you do go, and I get a call to come and pick you up halfway through, I will not look favorably on that, do you understand?"

Everyone nodded miserably. Gee didn't get angry very often, so it felt terrible when she did. It meant you'd done something really wrong: bad morals and threat to life or limb were the two things that really got Gee angry. The good news, though, about Gee's anger was that it always passed quickly, as it did now.

"Now, since I know that you girls will make a good choice

and behave admirably, we can put this subject to rest for the time being. Shall we drive or eat lunch first?"

It took the foursome a little bit longer to recover from their chastisement, but they gamely decided to drive first and eat later. Naturally, Neeve was first behind the wheel.

After a jerky start, and with Gee bracing her hand on the dashboard for self-defense, Neeve began inching down the driveway. The driving conditions were not ideal — the rain made it difficult to see and negotiating the windshield wipers was tricky, but little by little, Neeve got the feel for it. She'd driven golf carts before, around embassy properties and with her dad, playing golf, so she had a light touch on the gas and brake. The other three sat in the backseat, giggling and cheering her on. They couldn't wait for their own turns. Phoebe teased Neeve for being so tiny — she could hardly see over the steering wheel, but Gee coaxed her along gently and gave her simple instructions and confidence with her praise.

Within fifteen minutes or so, Neeve was smoothly cruising down the driveway, around, back up, and down again. Once Gee could see that they were in reasonably capable hands, she turned in her seat to give them all a little lecture on driving safety.

"Now, you all know that you should never, ever drive a car on the road, until you're a fully licensed and insured driver. The law does not look kindly on people who drive without the proper certification, and if you ever, God forbid, hurt anyone with a car while you were driving unlicensed or uninsured, you would feel horrible for life *and* your parents could get sued for every penny they have. The only time I could see it being okay for you to drive would be if there was an absolute state of emergency: a terrorist strike, or if someone has a heart attack in the middle of nowhere and there's no one else around. You would be forgiven for taking the wheel under such circumstances, which is why I'm teaching you now."

Gee announced a switch of drivers. ("Chinese fire drill!" called Neeve as she hopped out into the rain and ran around the car to Hillary's seat.) While Hillary took the wheel, Gee explained some of the finer points of driving, such as not tailgating, looking a few cars ahead to see what's coming up, and more. Hillary did well, and then it was on to Phoebe, who was fine, and Kate, who was a total disaster.

They were still laughing at Kate's incompetence when they finally finished driving school and went inside for lunch. Back in the kitchen, Sheila had a message for them. While they'd been driving, Sloan had called to remind them to bring their bathing suits on Saturday night, and the girls were thrilled that Sheila had informed Sloan that they were unavailable because they were out learning to drive.

"Oh, I wish I could've seen her face when you told her, Sheila!" laughed Neeve.

"She was plenty surprised, I'd say," said Sheila with a wink.

"I hope she's not one of those girls who makes a sleepover into a big production and always wants to talk about it and boss people around," sighed Kate.

"You know she is," said Phoebe.

"Wait, are we still going?" asked Hillary.

"I kind of think we have to," said Kate morosely. "I mean, we told her we'd be there. It seems too mean to bag."

Neeve had to agree. "But at least we'll be there together. Cousins forever!" This was their slogan, and it was the cue for the four of them to stack their fists on top of one another, lining up their white rope sailors' bracelets. "Cousins forever!" the others echoed.

CHAPTER SIX

The Sleepover

Saturday was golden warm and sunny, and after a day at the beach, the girls came home all salty and sandy to shower and pack up their overnight bags. Three calls had come in from Sloan since her mid-week bathing suit reminder: she wanted them each to bring a sleeping bag, some makeup, and something to trade. The girls were baffled by the trade concept, but figured it must be a New England tradition, so they each brought a piece of beaded jewelry they'd made that week.

Gee was at a baby shower tea, so at five o'clock, Sheila dropped them off in her rusty old Wagoneer. They grabbed their stuff from the back and walked up the path to the Bickets' door while Sheila pulled away. The house was in South Wing, the end of the island near town, where the more modest homes of the year-round people were, but the Bickets' house was actually elegant: tall, narrow, and imposing — a weathered gray saltbox with white trim, a white picket fence, and window boxes, all very neatly kept. It sat close to the street and the brick sidewalk, and the end of the street dead-ended at the cliffs above the ocean and some rocks below. The house reminded Neeve of an old, pinched spinster in starched clothes.

The girls rang the bell and waited. No one came. Neeve glanced around; the deep green lawn was so perfectly trimmed it looked as if each blade had been cut by hand with a nail scissors. After a moment, the girls decided they should just walk in; maybe Sloan was out back and hadn't heard them. Neeve pulled open the screen door and shouted, "Hello?!" But there was no answer. They inched into the hallway, calling, "Hello? Hello?" Alongside the staircase, there was a spindly antique bench with a hard seat, and opposite it, a long hall table with big square nails visible at the joints. Neeve could tell by its wear and tear that the table was also an antique, but it looked like it had been made by a cruel and unrefined black-smith rather than the fussy woodworker who'd made the bench. Neeve peeked into the dining room and living room as they passed and all was equally austere and uncozy-looking, and also neat as a pin. It looked more like a museum of New England's olden days than a family house where people actually lived.

The girls wandered toward the back of the house, through the dark wood kitchen — where clunky ceramic bowls of snacks were laid out in a straight line, obviously in wait for the party — and out the back door to the pool area.

"Sloan?" they called when they reached the terrace. "Sloan?"

"This is weird," said Phoebe.

"She must be around here somewhere. Maybe she's in the bathroom," suggested Kate.

Neeve laughed. "Working on her self-tanner?" she said in a whisper.

They put their things down on a hard wooden chaise and perched tentatively on the blocky wood chairs next to each other. They didn't think it was right to act too comfortable without their hostess there.

Neeve looked around the yard. The pool was a free-form shape, with landscaping around it and dark green water to make it look natural, like a pond. She was sure it was clean, but it didn't look inviting and fresh, like Gee's bright blue pool. The terrace was slate and also made to look natural, like it just happened to be there, but perfectly so, and the rest of the yard was more or less empty, save for the tightly clipped hedge that surrounded the impeccable grass. *Do kids really live here?* wondered Neeve.

Suddenly, up to their left, the door to the garage apartment opened with a bang, and Sloan came running down the stairs, grinning and flushed. "Hi! Sorry!" she called over the spiky, white picket fence that separated the driveway from the yard. "Be right there!"

"Of course," Neeve whispered wryly, rolling her eyes. "Tucker."

Their handsome sailing instructor, Tucker Hill, was lodging in the Bickets' garage apartment for the summer, and Sloan acted like this gave her ownership of him. She was forever dragging him aside, bossing him around, calling him "Tucky," and generally behaving in an annoying way that implied that she and he were, maybe, just a tiny bit more than friends. *As if,* the Callahans always said. He's seventeen and she's twelve, plus he's nice and she's a jerk. He put up with it all because he *was* such a nice guy, and, after all, the Bickets were his landlords. But the Callahans knew that Sloan bugged him.

Sloan came swinging through the white gate from the driveway, wearing a white string bikini top and apple green short-shorts. Her dark green eyes were flashing and her even white teeth gleamed in a smile in her overly tanned face.

"Hi," she said.

"Hi," the girls replied. "We couldn't find you," added Kate, needlessly.

"Oh, I was just, you know, hanging with Tuck," Sloan waved her hand airily toward the garage. But she very subtly raised her eyebrows and smiled, as if to imply that something interesting had been going on up there.

She was probably up there bugging him, thought Neeve in mild irritation. And just then, Tucker came out the door and tromping down the stairs, his hair wet and his clothes neat and clean. Sloan turned to glance at him and looked back at the Callahans, grinning like a cat. She clearly wanted them to think she'd been hanging out in there while he showered or something.

Tucker waved and, when he reached the driveway, crossed over to hang across the gate. "Hi, cousins!" he said with a smile. "Are you all geared up for the big sleepover?"

The girls greeted him and chatted for a minute; then he said, "Well, I'm off on my date! See you later!" and turned to go.

Sloan's face darkened and a scowl appeared. Tucker was ruining her illusions, but Neeve was giddy with happiness that he was going out with someone else. Now there would be no way for Sloan to drop inaccurate hints all night about some imagined budding romance with Tucker. "Have fun!" Neeve called after him. "Don't forget to walk her to her door!"

They could hear Tucker's laughter echoing back to them from the driveway, and then he was gone. Sloan was clearly annoyed that she'd lost control of the situation. She put her hands on her hips. "So," she said, to change the subject. "Did you bring your suits?"

Obviously, thought Neeve. *You made a special phone call just to remind us.*

"Yup, we did," said Kate brightly. It seemed Neeve and Kate were doing all the talking. Phoebe was mute with annoyance at being there and Hillary was so deeply suspicious of Sloan that she couldn't let down her guard to say anything at all.

"So go change!" ordered Sloan.

"Okay, um, where?" asked Kate.

"Just go into the kitchen and there's a bathroom off the mudroom. I'll wait here. Oh, actually, I'll get the snacks and bring them out," added Sloan.

They all trooped into the house, and the girls changed. The bathroom was kind of fake old-fashioned, with a wooden toilet seat and a flusher that you had to pull a chain to work. Sloan was waiting for them by the pool when they returned. But she looked them over in dismay.

"Where are your bikinis?" she asked. The cousins looked around. They were all wearing tank suits — Hillary's was even a racing suit. Not glamorous, but the best for pool games and fun.

"Why?" asked Neeve.

"Well, they're so much more . . . mature. I mean, tanks are for little kids. I thought I specifically said to bring a bikini." Sloan sighed heavily. "Sheila probably got it all wrong, the old goat," she muttered.

"Hey! That's not nice! We love Sheila!" Phoebe had finally found her voice.

"Well she's my aunt, so I can say whatever I want. And she is an old goat."

Hillary and Neeve glanced at each other. This might be the beginning of a very long and unpleasant evening, they seemed to be silently acknowledging.

"Anyway, I have loads of bikinis you can borrow. My mother lets me get ten new ones each summer — one for every week of vacation. I'll go get them." Sloan stood to go back into the house.

"Actually —," Neeve stopped her. "We're just grand in our own suits. Once we're in the pool it won't matter one bit what we're wearing."

Sloan froze and stared at her. "You want to go *in* the pool?" she asked in genuine surprise. "My friends and I *never* go *in* the pool."

Hillary laughed in shock. "So what do you do in your bathing suits?" she asked.

"Hang out. Work on our tans. Talk. You know." Sloan shrugged. "The usual."

"Are any of your other friends coming?" asked Phoebe.

"Yes, I'm expecting a few more people. But not until later."

"So then, what does it matter what the other people would do? Why don't we all just jump in and play some games for now?" suggested Hillary.

"Games! Games are for babies," said Sloan witheringly.

"Um, we don't think so," said Hillary.

Neeve could feel the tension gathering with every moment, so she did the first thing that popped into her mind. "Last one in is a rotten egg!" she cried, and she jumped sideways into the deep end. When she surfaced, the others had joined her, and Sloan was standing helplessly at the edge.

"Well, if that's what you really want to do . . ." she trailed off.

Neeve grinned. She'd just won a round for the Callahans. "Yes! Come on in! The water's great!"

Sloan hesitated a moment longer; then finally she nodded. "Alright. But I have to go change out of this bathing suit. It's see-through when it gets wet." She turned to go inside and when she emerged a moment later she, too, was wearing a tank suit.

The late afternoon and early evening actually passed pleasantly after the rocky start. Sloan loosened up a bit and had fun playing pool games, and when they got out for a break they all gorged on the snacks she'd arranged. Neeve wasn't a huge fan of health food — junk was her mainstay, since at least it was always packaged and you knew what you were getting, whether you were in Shanghai or Dublin — but the dry pretzels, trail mix, and dried apricots at least gave her back some of the energy she'd spent in the pool.

The really weird part, though, for Neeve, was that there were no grown-ups around. She was used to her mum and dad always being home when she had friends over for a sleepover; and it wasn't only because they thought that it was the responsible and hospitable thing to do: they really liked her friends. Her mum would always spend a bit with them, her legs curled girlishly under her, and debate the merits of various pop stars versus others. And her dad would charge in with platters of food, or pop in to scare them before they went to sleep. Her parents really enjoyed having her friends around. And her friends felt it, and Neeve felt it, and it always made for happy gatherings, no matter what country they were in. It was the same at The Sound; Gee was always there to meet their friends and get to know them, and that was a cozy, secure feeling.

But there hadn't been a sign of Sloan's parents — or even a

nanny or an amah, like Neeve had always had in Asia — no grown-up was there at all. It kind of freaked Neeve out, and she worried about what Gee would say if she knew. Apparently, Sloan's parents and little brother ("The Pest," Sloan called him) were out on a sailing picnic and wouldn't be home until nine o'clock or so, but they'd called ahead for pizzas to be delivered at seven, which must've been a huge treat for Sloan, based on how excited she was about it.

They'd set up their pizza out by the pool in their bathing suits, and as they were about to eat, three other guests arrived. There was Lark, the pretty Japanese girl from sailing clinic, and Anna, who was silent and sometimes came to sailing, and Jessie, who had curly red hair and frightened blue eyes. Without the girls expressly saying so, it became clear that they were late because they'd all been waiting for Lark to come back from Woods Hole with her parents. None of them had wanted to arrive alone.

So everyone ate the pizza together, with Sloan dominating the conversation. The three late arrivals seemed alternately terrified and thrilled to be there, but Neeve did notice a certain spark in Lark's eye that indicated she might be more fun than she seemed. (That made Neeve like her the best.) Otherwise, Neeve wasn't sure what Sloan could get out of friendships with the others — they all just agreed with her and laughed at her jokes, but they didn't share anything interesting about themselves, or tell any good stories or jokes, or anything. They didn't even seem to have opinions — even on TV shows. They just waited to see what Sloan had to say and then nodded. *No wonder she wants new friends!* thought Neeve.

After dinner it grew chilly, so they decided to go up to Sloan's room. Sloan instructed everyone to bring their gear upstairs, and the Callahans ducked into the bathroom one by one to change out of their swimsuits. Then Sloan announced that it was makeover time, and would everyone please lay out their makeup so she could see what they had to work with.

Neeve presented her bulging makeup bag with a flourish. She was way into cosmetics and had a fascinating collection of them amassed during her travels all over the world. Sloan was truly impressed, and she cozied right up to Neeve as Neeve laid everything out and explained what it was for.

"And this is rice powder from Japan," said Neeve, gently touching a high-tech compact. "It evens out your complexion and makes you look really pale, which they're super-into over there."

Lark nodded and seemed to be about to say something, but Sloan cut in.

"And what's this one?" she demanded, hefting each item in her hand as if she were considering it for purchase.

Neeve picked up the small, unmarked pot filled with brick-red colored stuff that Sloan had indicated. "It's Masai war paint, from Kenya. My best friend's dad was the, like, witch doctor in their tribe, so he used to make it. He always said the red color came from lions' blood, but I never believed him."

"Ew!" Sloan dropped the pot as if it had burned her, and Neeve laughed. The other three visitors looked shocked, while Phoebe and Kate seemed repulsed. Hillary was intrigued, of course, so she picked it up for inspection.

"It's not true, anyway! Lions are protected now. No one kills them anymore. It's probably, like, rat blood or something." Neeve wanted to drag the teasing out even further, and it worked. Sloan shuddered. Neeve knew perfectly well that it was just red clay that Jomo dug up in his rose garden behind his house in Nairobi. But it was actually pretty fun to torture Sloan.

Sloan turned to the more European-looking stuff in Neeve's collection, and continued with her questions. Meanwhile, the others were getting restless. Kate had a small sampling of good-old American drugstore cosmetics laid out in front of her, but Sloan wasn't particularly interested in those. Phoebe had just her mascara (which she'd worn since the third grade when a mean boy in her class began calling her "Bald Eye" because of her fair eyelashes) and one blue eyeliner, and Hillary only had lip balm (she wasn't into makeup at all). Lark, Jessie, and Anna had all "forgotten" their makeup, which made Neeve mildly suspicious of Sloan's intentions.

In any case, the others were quickly growing bored of Sloan's fascination with Neeve's things.

"Want to go grab sodas?" whispered Hillary to the group. Jessie, Anna, and Lark glanced at Sloan for permission, but she was too engrossed to notice.

"Sure," said Phoebe. Everyone rose to go downstairs, and Neeve and Sloan hardly looked up to see them go.

"And what's this one?" continued Sloan, holding up a small silver compact with a green enameled shamrock on it.

Neeve laughed. "Oh, that's some perfume balm from Ireland. My mum's mum gave it to me. It's kind of old-ladyish but I like the compact and the idea of hard perfume that you rub on."

Sloan snapped it open for a whiff. "My dad was at your dad's wedding, you know."

She'd said it in such an offhand manner that Neeve could scarcely believe her ears. But her stomach clutched and a chill went over her, so she knew she hadn't been mistaken. "Oh, really?" Neeve tried to play it casually, keep the panic out of her voice. "In Ireland?" she asked.

Sloan looked up at her sharply. "No. Here, silly."

"Right. Just kidding." Neeve could hardly breathe. Sloan clearly didn't know anything about the mystery wedding. She'd just assumed it was when Neeve's dad had married Neeve's mum.

"Yeah," Sloan continued, rubbing a little of the perfume on her wrist and then waving her wrist in the air. "I've seen pictures of it, around, you know, in a file or something."

Neeve nearly died on the spot. But the last thing she could do was let Sloan know she had any powerful information in her possession. Coolly, Neeve said, "Wow. I'd love to see them sometime."

"Sure, I could probably dig those out," said Sloan. She took a whiff of her wrist and wrinkled her nose. "Yuck, you're right. It smells like my grandmother."

Remain calm, Neeve told herself. *Remain calm. Just because there are photos of your father's wedding to another woman in the very house you are in, there is no need to freak out.*

Hillary and the gang tumbled in just then, organic juice pouches in hand. They glanced at Neeve, then did a double-take. Neeve knew the shock must be plain on her face, because the cousins all looked sharply at Sloan, as if she'd done something to Neeve in their absence.

"Everything okay up here?" ventured Hillary. She looked warily back and forth between Neeve and Sloan.

Sloan looked up, truly innocent for perhaps the first time in her life. "Yeah. Why?"

Hillary glanced at Neeve, but Neeve shook her head just the tiniest bit, as if telling Hillary not to pursue it. Thankfully, Hillary got the picture and backed off. "Oh, no reason. We just didn't want you to miss us while we were gone."

Just then, the phone rang. Sloan ran to get it and returned to say her parents were having trouble getting their boat started and were going to try to split up and hitch rides on other people's boats to get home. Sloan was nonplussed, but apparently her mother had told her she would try to track down Tucker on his cell phone to see if he'd bring his date by and check in on the girls. Neeve thought it was a bit strange that there wasn't anyone else in the extended Bicket family or friend network who could be called upon to check in on them. Couldn't Mrs. Bicket call anyone for a favor besides their summer lodger?

"Anyway, good luck," Sloan was laughing. "If I know Tuck, he's got a whole lot more on his mind right now than babysitting. My mom'll be lucky if his phone is even on!" The others smiled uncomfortably, and no one responded to her implied intimate knowledge of what Tucker did on dates.

"So. We could do the makeovers, then watch a movie, and, afterwards do our trading," said Sloan decisively. "Oh, and when we go down for the movie, I'll try to find those photos for you," Sloan said, turning to Neeve and smiling warmly. She was now so impressed by Neeve's makeup and worldliness that she was acting eager-to-please and very un-Sloan-like.

The others looked at Sloan and then at Neeve.

"What photos?" asked Phoebe.

Sloan began to answer, "We have these old photos from Neeve's parents' . . ."

"Just silly stuff," interrupted Neeve brightly. She didn't want the others to know anything about it, and she truly wished Sloan hadn't said anything in front of them. She had to change the subject immediately. "Now can I go first for the makeover? Pretty please with sugar on top?" she said charmingly. But she caught both Phoebe and Hillary looking at her suspiciously, and she knew they were going to end up finding out about her dad's mystery sooner than she'd hoped.

CHAPTER SEVEN

Family Albums

The girls sat on the rag-rug-covered floor in Sloan's chilly den, fully made-up, as if they were going to a prom or even — as Hillary pointed out — a Halloween party. Neeve wanted to laugh every time she looked at Hillary; she was so unused to seeing her with makeup on. But she was so quivery nervous about Sloan's photos that she couldn't even muster a smile. Plus, if she laughed, she knew that Hillary would just feel awful and go wash it all off.

Kate looked like a little girl who'd gotten into her mother's makeup bag. Her lips were outlined far outside their natural line, giving her a clownish appearance, and the eyeliner Sloan had applied was thick and too dark. Lark and the others had not particularly interested Sloan, so they'd gotten by with just a dusting of eyeshadow and a slash of lipgloss. But Phoebe, on the other hand, had been transformed. She actually looked like a model, Neeve thought. Phoebe'd even seemed to realize it when Sloan had finished the application. There had been a big pause — like everyone in the room was holding her breath — while Phoebe looked at the result in the mirror. When they saw the pleased look on her face and heard her barely audible "Wow," the others had burst into spontaneous applause. She looked amazing, and Neeve was happy for her and surprised. *Who knew the old bookworm had it in her?* she thought with a giggle.

Now, as *Mean Girls* started up on the DVD player, Neeve shifted nervously on the uncomfortably lumpy rug. She wanted to ask Sloan to look for the photos, but she didn't want the others to know. She hesitated for a minute until it seemed that at least her cousins were engrossed, then she leaned over to Sloan to whisper, "Hey, I'd love to see those pictures if you have them around somewhere."

"Hmmm?" Sloan was engrossed, too, which Neeve hadn't anticipated. "Oh, but I love this part." She turned to look at Neeve. "Why don't you just go look for them and bring them back in here? There's a filing basket on that bookcase in the living room."

"Okay." This was even better, even if there was no way she'd bring them back in there, where all of her cousins sat. Neeve stood up abruptly and the others glanced at her, distracted. She motioned that she'd be right back and they turned back to the television.

Quickly, she slid into the living room and clicked on the lights. She immediately saw the basket. She crossed the room, lifted it down, and sat heavily on the uncarpeted plank floor so as not to mess up the perfectly squared-off pillows on the couch. She flicked quickly through the files inside. The first one was fruitless, just old fliers and programs; and then the second was the same. It felt weird to be going through someone else's family mementos — particularly when that family was enemies with her family. Or had been. Whatever.

There were some photos tucked in here and there, and Neeve eagerly seized them, only to be disappointed each time when they were not what she was seeking. But besides her growing anxiety at not finding the pictures, Neeve was also shocked that none of these photos were in albums or frames, as far as she could see. It was a little weird; the whole house looked as if no one lived there, and then there was this sparse little basket with maybe three handfuls of snapshots, and that was it. Neeve's own homes were always loaded with photos of the family and their friends, and Gee was practically obsessed with family photos. Well, maybe the Bickets just weren't into . . .

"Jackpot!" breathed Neeve almost silently.

There, in about eight brightly colored photographs, was her father, marrying someone else. There was no denying it this time, no convincing herself otherwise. Her dad and this girl (really, she looked so young) were walking down the aisle holding hands, dancing under a tent, kissing! Kissing! Neeve thought she might actually be sick.

Just then, Sloan's front door opened and Neeve nearly

jumped out of her skin. She slammed the file shut guiltily, but it was only Tucker and Gina, the nice waitress from The Snack, which was the lunch counter at Macaroni Beach.

"Hi," gulped Neeve.

"Hi," said Tucker, laughing all of a sudden. "You look like you've just seen a ghost."

Neeve smiled weakly. She couldn't think of anything to say. All she could think was that she had to get these photos out of the Bickets' file and into her bag as quickly as possible.

"Everything okay?" asked Tucker, looking around the room. "Where's everyone else?" He very considerately did not ask what Neeve was doing, even though it must've looked kind of suspicious.

"In there, watching *Mean Girls*. But I've seen it, like, ten times already," said Neeve.

Gina laughed. "I'm kind of over it, too. I think I saw it three times in the theater myself." Gina was nice and Neeve was grateful.

"I'm just going to poke my head in there and say hi," said Tucker. "The Bickets should be home any minute."

"I'll go with you," offered Gina.

Phew! thought Neeve. *Here's my chance!*

She flipped open the file again, and began looking for a way to get the photos out of there. She didn't have any pockets, so she thought maybe she could hide the photos under a cushion or something and come back to get them later. She didn't really feel like it was stealing, because the pictures were of her dad anyway, and it wasn't like the Bickets would ever notice they were gone.

But just as Neeve was lifting a couch cushion to tuck them under, Sloan walked in.

Sloan took one look at her and her face clouded. "Hey!" she said. "You can't *take* those!"

There was no use trying to hide what she was doing. So Neeve looked up, defeated, and simply said, "Sorry."

"Just put 'em back in like they were, okay?" said Sloan huffily. "I'm going to make popcorn." And she stalked off, down the hall to the kitchen.

Neeve was torn. She wanted the photos so badly but she knew that she couldn't take them now. As she reluctantly stuffed them back into the file, Lark walked through the room on her way to the bathroom. She gave Neeve a sympathetic if confused look, but she didn't stop to see if Neeve was okay. Neeve understood, though. It couldn't have been easy being stuck on Gull Island with Sloan all year long. You'd have to play by different rules. Her rules.

Neeve put the basket back on the shelf again, and with one last look, she turned to go back into the den.

By the time the movie ended, the Bickets had returned and Tucker had been released back onto his date. Sloan's parents were pleasant, but it was late, and no one was feeling particularly chatty.

The girls trooped up to Sloan's room to wash off their makeup in her bathroom, unroll their sleeping bags, and retire for the night. Sloan's parents had gone to their room, and her little brother was fast asleep — his dad had actually carried him in from the car and straight up to his bed, so the Callahans had never had a chance to meet him.

Now, in her sleeping bag, in the dark, Neeve was going crazy. All she could think about were the photos downstairs and how she'd never be able to spend any time studying them alone. She was desperate for more information about the whole thing, but she didn't feel ready yet to ask someone for the facts. It was like she wanted to come to her own conclusions from what she could glean from the photos, before she started asking any questions. If she could imagine the worst-case scenario, then the truth probably wouldn't be so bad. That was what she always did when she found out they were moving somewhere new. She'd go to the library or online and look up every bad thing about the place they were going, and then when they finally moved, the reality was always better than what she'd dreaded.

Sloan was still awake. Neeve could tell by her breathing. But she was pretty sure the others were fast asleep.

She took a deep breath. "Sloan?" she whispered.

"Yeah?" Sloan didn't sound sleepy at all.

"Um, did your dad ever tell you anything about my dad's wedding?"

Sloan whispered back. "Not much. Just that it was in a tent

at your grandmother's house, and they all drank too much, and it was really fun."

"Anything else?" Neeve whispered. "Like, about the bride?"

Sloan was getting suspicious. "No. Why?"

"What are you talking about?" Phoebe interrupted groggily. Neeve's stomach flipped. She'd been sure the others were asleep.

"Shh!" said Kate, half-asleep.

Neeve rolled over restlessly and tried to go to sleep. She lay there for about fifteen minutes until suddenly, she had a brainstorm.

"Hey, Sloan," she whispered. "We forgot to do our trades."

"Yeah," said Sloan, sleepy now.

"Maybe I could trade you something for the pictures?"

"Hmmmm," said Sloan.

Neeve couldn't tell if that was a yes or no, but she had to convince herself that it was a yes, or she'd never fall asleep.

CHAPTER EIGHT
Fair Trade

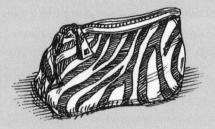

*A*t breakfast the next morning, Sloan began acting bratty. Neeve wasn't sure why, but maybe it was because the Callahans were talking about their stay at Gee's and all the fun they'd been having. Or maybe it was because they'd mentioned that they were moving down to the Dorm. Sloan had seemed jealous and almost angry, and then she'd started bossing her mom around, and barking orders at her brother to leave them alone, when he hadn't even shown the slightest interest in hanging around them. Her mother seemed embarrassed and acted stern with Sloan, which only made it worse. The Callahans began exchanging looks of discomfort over the breakfast pastries they'd brought as a gift, and finally Phoebe made up a story about needing to call Gee to come pick them up so they could be home in time for some family event. It was only nine-thirty in the morning, but the Callahans all felt they'd seen enough of Sloan for a while. Lark, Anna, and

Jessie didn't seem particularly unnerved by Sloan's behavior; they were probably used to it. But they seized on the Callahans' departure as a graceful way for them to exit, too.

Neeve was frantic, though. She didn't want to leave the house without the photos, but she also didn't want her cousins to find out about them. She felt almost ashamed that her father had been married before, and in some way, ashamed of herself for not knowing. The last thing she wanted was for Sloan to spill the beans.

But how could she start the whole trading thing without involving them? Could she just do some sort of a side trade with Sloan? What was this whole trading thing about anyway? Did Sloan want some makeup? The beaded jewelry she'd brought? She had no idea.

But she saw her chance when the others went upstairs to pack up their things. She hung back a tiny bit and grabbed Sloan at the foot of the stairs.

"Hey, we never did our trades!" she said brightly.

"Oh yeah, well, whatever," said Sloan, and she made a move to head upstairs.

Neeve grabbed her arm, almost desperately, and Sloan looked down at it with a withering look until Neeve released it.

"Sorry," said Neeve. "But, I was wondering if, um . . ."

Sloan tapped her foot impatiently. "Yes?"

"Would you ever want to trade like, something of mine for those photos?" Neeve let it all out in a rush. That was the only way.

The expression on Sloan's face changed from annoyed to puzzled, then to downright calculating. Neeve could practically see the gleam in Sloan's eye as Sloan mentally rifled through Neeve's makeup bag.

"Maybe," said Sloan, folding her arms and leaning back against the banister.

"Okay, like what?" Gee was due to arrive any second and Neeve still had to pack. She would've given Sloan anything to just get her to hand over the photos and be done with it.

Sloan looked at Neeve appraisingly. "The ring," she said.

Neeve gasped. "This?!" She looked down at the Irish Claddagh ring that Gee had given each of the girls earlier in the summer. It was a symbol of loyalty and love, and they all four wore them. There was no way Neeve could give hers to Sloan. It would be a mockery of the symbolism of the ring, not to mention a slap in the face to the cousins and Gee.

"Yes. That," said Sloan, nodding. Sloan had the smug look of someone who knew she was getting what she wanted.

But Neeve wasn't that desperate. "No," she said, looking Sloan right in the eye. "I can't give it to you."

"Why?" asked Sloan haughtily.

"Because Gee gave it to me, and we all have them."

"So have her get you a new one. Say you lost yours." Sloan really was devious.

Neeve actually considered it for a moment. But then she shook her head, as much to clear the thoughts from her mind as to refuse Sloan. "No. I can't."

"Then no photos," said Sloan, as if she couldn't care less. She turned on her heel and began walking up the stairs again.

"Wait!" Neeve cried in desperation, hardly realizing the word was out of her mouth.

Sloan waved her hand behind her as if to dismiss Neeve, and she kept climbing the stairs.

Neeve was nearly hysterical. She followed Sloan up into her room where the others were just finishing up their packing. Everyone looked up and was clearly confused; the looks on their faces said that they all knew they'd missed something.

Neeve smiled wanly at them and tried to think of how she could continue her deal-making without letting anything on to the others. She bent to roll her sleeping bag and pack up her things. But when she reached for her makeup bag, she hefted it in her hand and stopped, as if weighing it. Then, she quickly reached inside and slipped her grandmother's compact out and into her shorts pocket.

"Sloan?" she said.

Sloan turned from her dresser and looked at Neeve. Wordlessly, Neeve held out the bag to her.

Sloan cocked an eyebrow and looked at her, as if considering the offer. Then she reached for the bag and placed it on her dresser. "Tomorrow," she said. "I'll bring them to clinic."

Hillary, Phoebe, and Kate were mystified. "What's this all about?" Phoebe demanded indignantly. "Are you giving her your makeup?"

Sloan ignored the question.

Neeve shrugged. "Sloan really likes it, and I'm, um, kind of tired of it. I was thinking of buying a bunch of American makeup before I go back." She was trying to play it cool but the others weren't buying it. They knew how much Neeve loved her exotic stuff.

"But why?" insisted Kate.

"Oh, just as a thank-you present, for having us . . ." Neeve trailed off and finished her packing with a flourish. "Come on. Let's go! Gee's probably waiting already." She gathered her things and stepped out the door and down the stairs, with the others trailing behind her. Lark and her buddies had watched the whole scene in silence. *They're really like extras in a movie,* Neeve thought distractedly. *Just warm bodies to fill up a room. They're not Sloan's friends at all.*

"But you didn't need to do that!" insisted Kate in a whisper. "We brought those pastries and things! At least let us all contribute something. You don't have to give her your whole bag!"

But Neeve waved her hand dismissively at Kate as Sloan had only moments before waved at Neeve. She knew it was mean but she wanted the subject closed. If she dwelled too much on it, she would regret it. Better to not think about it.

"Let's move on, shall we?" said Neeve brightly, as she wheeled to face Kate and the others on the stairs.

The others stared at her long and hard. Neeve knew that they knew she was up to something, but she could tell they had no idea what. Finally, they seemed to give in. Phoebe shrugged. "Whatever," she said. And they all trotted wordlessly down the stairs and around the corner into the kitchen.

Sloan appeared a moment later while they were saying their goodbyes and thank-yous to the Bickets. The girls all said a nice goodbye and thank you to her, too, but Phoebe, Kate, and Hillary looked at her warily. They knew she was up to no good, but if Neeve wasn't willing to fill them in, then there was nothing they could do about it.

Just then they heard the asthmatic wheeze of Gee's Volvo as it pulled up and idled by the curb. With a final farewell, they left the Bickets and trooped out to the car. Sloan stood in the doorway and waved them off, but Neeve didn't look back.

While Gee peppered them with questions about the evening (they, naturally, omitted the fact that they had been left alone and unsupervised for the better part of the sleepover), Neeve looked out the window, turning only occasionally to answer questions with a vague yes or no.

When they got back to The Sound, Kate wanted everyone to work on the Dorm for a little while. The experience at the Bickets' had made them feel more united than ever, so they all agreed to Kate's idea. But even as they hustled down there and divided up the work, Neeve was distracted. She wondered if Sloan would really bring the photos to clinic, as she had promised. She thought about her whole collection of cosmetics and how she had willingly offered it, like some sacrificial lamb, to Sloan, when probably one or two items would have been enough. And all for some photos that, in actuality, she really didn't want to see. The first thing she'd do after she got the photos from Sloan was figure out how she could get most — if not all — of her cosmetics back.

Down at the Dorm, when no one was looking, Neeve slipped out of the loft, onto the porch, and up the ladder to the lookout tower. From this perch, she could see exactly where a wedding tent would have fit in Gee's yard; just to the left of the house, before the lawn began its slope down to the water. She pictured Gee at the wedding: younger, radiant, and then she pictured Pops, happy and proud as the father of the groom. She imagined the strains of music from the band, and cooking smells from the caterers, and cars lining the driveway and the street. And her dad in a tux. With that girl.

She slumped down inside the tower and leaned back against the wooden wall. Through a weird trick of acoustics, she could now hear everything that the others were saying, down on the first floor.

First they called her. "Neeve? Neeve? Where are you?"

Then they discussed the idea that she might have gone back up to the house for some coffee. Then, when they'd finally decided that she wasn't there, they began discussing her strange behavior at the sleepover the previous night and this morning. Neeve strained her ears to catch every word.

"But they kept talking about photos," Kate was insisting.

"And she definitely said something about a wedding. I know it." Phoebe was standing firm.

"I'm sure she'll tell us when she's ready," said Hillary rationally. Neeve smiled a small smile. She could always count on Hillary to be calm and collected.

"I don't know. It sounded like Sloan was dangling something over her head." Phoebe liked to analyze all the angles of things.

"I just hope she's okay," said Kate worriedly.

"I'm sure she's fine," said Hillary. "And when she wants to tell us, she'll tell us."

"Well if she doesn't tell us in the next day or two, I'm asking!" declared Phoebe.

"You go, girl!" Hillary teased.

"I will!" said Phoebe emphatically.

Neeve sighed. She really had great cousins. What would she do without them as a sort of home base? She felt herself relaxing from the stress of being around Sloan and being at that uncomfortable and rather unfriendly house. Now that she was home, she could finally let her guard down and just be normal.

But *uh-oh!* Kate was down there now, directing the others in her decorating plans. Neeve could hear the words "white" and "Ralph Lauren-ish" rising up through the rafters. She had to get down there pronto before that girl took over! She squared her tiny shoulders, slapped a smile across her pale, freckled face, and headed down the ladder. No need for them to think she was upset or anything.

CHAPTER NINE

The Promised Land

Neeve dropped her bike and raced into Hagan's Marina Monday morning; her legs were burning from pedaling so fast, but she ignored the discomfort. She scanned the room, looking for Sloan, as the other cousins trailed in behind her with bewildered looks on their faces. She knew they were wondering what her obsession with Sloan was, but she was too focused on the outcome of her trade to care.

Where was Sloan?! Neeve was practically vibrating with impatience. Oh! It was so frustrating! Just leave it to Sloan to drag this out, she thought.

Finally, she could wait no longer. They were all called to assemble into their groups and Neeve had to join hers, even though Sloan had not yet appeared. But all during the start of their lesson, Neeve was craning her head to see if Sloan had arrived, and finally Tucker made a joke about it.

"Huh?" said Neeve, startled when she heard her name. Everyone was laughing.

"Expecting someone?" said Tucker again with a smile.

But Neeve wasn't one to be teased without giving it right back. "Oh, I heard that your new girlfriend might stop by and I wanted the chance to tell her how much we all enjoyed meeting her the other night during your date." Neeve grinned, and the rest of the group hooted and stamped their feet. Neeve had won that one. Tucker smiled and turned pink, but he didn't back down either.

"I'm sure she enjoyed babysitting you all." He probably thought that was enough of a put-down, but Neeve saw it as a set-up for one last zinger.

She was laughing now. "Yeah, that must've been a *really* special evening out for her. Remind me to call you whenever I need dating advice!"

"Alright, alright! That's enough. Back to sailing!" insisted Tucker, before the group got totally out of hand.

But Neeve was feeling better now. Nothing like a good dose of teasing to restore her to her usual equilibrium. And, in fact, when she turned one last time, she saw that Sloan had arrived. Phew. Now it would only be a short while before she got the photos.

⛵

But Neeve's path did not cross Sloan's until clinic let out at noon. As soon as Tucker freed them, Neeve raced across the room, puzzled cousins in her wake, and practically jumped on Sloan.

"Hiya, Sloanie! Got my pictures?" she asked breathlessly.

"What?" replied Sloan.

Neeve's heart sank, and her confidence went with it. "Um, the pictures? You know, that I traded you all of my makeup for? Did you bring them?"

Sloan looked at her with disdain as understanding dawned on her face. "Oh. Those. Well. The trade wasn't complete," she said, and she tossed her hair.

Neeve was aghast. "What do you mean? You didn't bring them?"

"No," said Sloan. "The compact was missing from the makeup bag, and until I get that . . ." She snapped her fingers. "No pictures." She turned and began to walk toward the door, but Neeve jumped in front of her.

"Wait! I can't give you that compact. It belonged to my grandmother. It's an heirloom!" Neeve was near tears, and she only vaguely noticed as the other cousins approached them.

"Tough. No deal, then."

Sloan was ruthless, and Neeve felt her usual charm and composure melting away. She wasn't above pleading with Sloan. But she drew herself upright and summoned up all of her courage. "Then give me back my makeup," she said nervously.

But Sloan looked at her in disgust. "I'll look into it," she said, and stalked off.

"Look into it?" muttered Neeve as she collapsed on a couch in a daze.

Phoebe stepped in front of her with her hands on her hips like a drill sergeant. "Alright, Callahan!" she barked. "What on earth is going on here? Tell us this instant!"

Neeve rested her head in her hands. She didn't want to tell them, but she was beginning to feel like she was in over her head. She peeked out between her fingers and saw Kate, who was practically wringing her hands, and Hillary, whose face was rigid with worry. And Phoebe, who looked furious, actually.

Neeve had to laugh in spite of herself. "Phoebe! Why are you so mad?!"

Phoebe's face softened just a bit. "I'm not mad at you. I'm mad at Sloan. And . . . I'm . . ." Neeve was beginning to wonder if Phoebe was so used to reading about *other* people's feelings that she was never sure what she herself was feeling. After a pause, Phoebe began again. "Actually, I am mad at you. There's something serious going on between you and Sloan and you're leaving us out. And I'm worried about you, and I'm mad that you won't let us in on it so we can help you. So there!"

All three of the other cousins burst out laughing. "Wow!" said Kate. "You sound like Dr. Phil on *Oprah!*"

"Thanks, Bee," said Neeve. "I'm touched." She grinned.

"So then 'fess up," ordered Phoebe.

Neeve sighed. She really hadn't wanted to get the others in on it — especially not before she'd had time to do a little asking around herself. And even more than that, she didn't like to be a downer — complaining about her worries, when everyone had their own stuff to worry about. Neeve always preferred to keep up a happy-go-lucky front. But there was no way out of this one now; if she didn't tell them herself, they'd find it all out from Sloan sooner or later. And, she had to admit it finally, it *would* be so much better if she had people to discuss it with. That's what cousins were for, really.

"Alright, let's make a deal. We'll go home, pick up lunch from Sheila, and go for a picnic at the Promised Land. I'll tell you there."

"Is this just another strategy to throw us off the scent?" asked Hillary skeptically.

"No. I promise," said Neeve. And she smiled her most sincere smile.

By the time they got back to The Sound, they were famished and hot, and Sheila told them to go dunk in the pool while she put a picnic together. When they returned, she had packed everything into a soft, ancient tote bag; then she shooed them out the door, insisting that they were dripping all over her clean kitchen floor.

"Thanks, Sheila!" Neeve called, blowing kisses over her shoulder.

"Off then, with the lot of yas!" scolded Sheila in her Irish accent, but they all knew she was only joking.

The "Promised Land" was the name that the Callahan family had jokingly given to an adorable little cove at the back end of the property. Getting there required a fairly arduous trek across the side yard, through some woods, past the Fallen Down Trees — where the girls had liked to play pirates and house when they were little — through a small wildflower meadow, and down to the rocky coastline below. But when one arrived there, the scene was so picturesque — a tiny sandy beach with a shallow, clear inlet for swimming — that it was immediately obvious that the name wasn't really a joke. It was an especially dear place for the girls because it was where Callahan children and grandchildren were traditionally taught to swim. And as the children grew older, visits there took on a certain significance since it wasn't a piece of cake to get to, and finding it on your own, without an adult, was something of an accomplishment. It hadn't been a surprise to the others when Neeve had suggested this very place for her big revelation.

The girls were famished when they finally reached the spot, and they could hardly wait for Kate to lay out the blanket and distribute the food. There were chicken salad sandwiches, cucumber sandwiches, and tomato sandwiches, all with the crusts cut off. Sheila had tucked in four hardboiled eggs with a little wax paper twist full of salt for dipping, and there were four little sacks of potato chips. At the bottom of the bag was a thermos of iced tea and some plastic cups, and a little box filled with chocolate chip cookies that Sheila had just made from scratch. With such an amazing spread before them, there was no question of discussing Neeve's crisis until they had eaten.

But at long last, they leaned back against the big rocks, in little nooks worn soft by years of erosion, and listened while Neeve began explaining everything, just as she had promised.

At first, Neeve hadn't been sure whether she should drop a big bombshell, like, "My dad was married before," right off the bat just to get it over with, or whether she should ease them into it. On the walk to the cove, she'd decided on the more cautious strategy. It didn't sound as harsh.

"You remember that day, when I got heatstroke in the attic?" she began. "Well, I don't think it was really heatstroke. It was more like shock, I think."

The others listened attentively as she explained that she'd seen a photograph of something really surprising, and then she'd hidden it, only to return to find it missing. Then, she went on, after being tortured for days by what she'd seen, she discovered that Sloan had photographs of the same thing. So she'd been trading and begging and trying to get them from Sloan ever since.

By this point in the story, the others girls were on the edges of their seats — or rocks, actually. They couldn't imagine what had been in the photographs, but they knew Neeve was getting to that. Finally, after all the facts of the timeline and the conflict with Sloan had been laid out, Neeve took a deep breath.

"So, do you want to know what the photo was of?" she asked quietly.

The others nodded their heads, too wrapped up in the suspense to even speak.

Neeve sat up straight and looked each of them in the eye,

one by one. And then she said, "It was a wedding picture of my dad. Only he wasn't marrying my mum in it." And she sat back against her rock.

"Oh my God!" yelled Phoebe, who had been totally engrossed in the story.

"Are you sure?" asked Hillary, leaning forward. Her parents had recently split up, so she was especially attuned to marital issues these days.

"What do you mean?" asked Kate, who looked confused. "How could he be married to two people?"

Kate's comment broke the heaviness of the moment, and they all laughed when Phoebe called her a "mindless twit."

"Duh!" said Neeve. "He was married before!"

"Oh!" Kate's eyes were huge with wonder. "Wow!"

"So why do you need those pictures so badly?" asked Phoebe.

" 'Cause I thought I could learn more about it, or about her, from the photos, maybe." Now Neeve wasn't so sure. "And, I thought they'd help me get used to the idea, before I had to ask Gee or my dad for the facts."

"Hey, we can get the facts ourselves!" Phoebe was indignant. "We don't need to ask any grown-ups! We can just go to the library and look it up. I mean, if they were married on Gull, it must be in the town records, or the church records, or there might've been an announcement in the paper or something."

"Oh yeah!" said Neeve. Duh, herself! Why hadn't she thought of that?

"Yeah, and there might also be some pictures in the family albums, downstairs in the main house," offered Hillary. She had spent her fair share of time picking through them; she'd had to make sure she was fully represented, now that her parents had split and she was living with her mom (whom Hillary had decided wasn't technically a Callahan anymore).

"We could even go back up to the attic and look for some more," said Kate, who was always angling for more time up there.

Neeve felt a wave of gratitude wash over her. "You guys are the best. I feel better already!" She smiled at them. How could she have even hesitated to tell them about this? She shook her head at her own stupidity.

"So when should we start?" asked Phoebe, reaching for another cookie.

Neeve grabbed one, too, and munched thoughtfully. "I guess as soon as possible. I really am dying for facts, now that I'm slightly used to the idea."

Kate stood and came to crouch next to Neeve. She put her arm around Neeve's shoulder and gave her a tight squeeze. "You know, you should have told us sooner."

"I know." Neeve nodded.

"Are you alright?" asked Hillary.

"Yes, actually. I'm quite good!" And Neeve hopped up to splash in the cove to prove it. Her confession had made her feel lighter than air, and she was ready to enjoy that long-lost sensation.

CHAPTER TEN

Bits and Pieces

With the big "reveal" of the Dorm planned for Sunday, the girls had their hands full. Now, with clinic every day plus their mission to help Neeve, it was all they could do to get in a coat of paint or a floor waxing in between sailing and research. And Kate was getting frustrated.

"Listen, guys, we really need to buckle down and get this done!" Kate was saying by Wednesday. "I mean, the Uncle Bill thing isn't going anywhere. It doesn't matter if we postpone all that for just a few more days. Gee's going to lose all faith in us if we don't finish on schedule!"

But Phoebe and Hillary had looked at her like she was nuts, and Neeve had been grateful to them and more annoyed than ever with Kate. And off they'd gone, Phoebe to the town library and Hillary to Gee's home library, to continue their research. Feeling guilty for pulling them away from the tasks at hand, Neeve reluctantly allowed herself to be bossed around by Kate a bit. And as the week wore on, the two of them actually made quite a bit of progress with the basics.

Hillary and Phoebe were not as quick. Hillary had zipped through all the albums on the first day, before she got claustrophobia and had to go outdoors, but sifting through Gee's stored boxes of photos was taking quite a bit longer. The pictures were all lumped in randomly: 1936 and 1996 were often found in the same box. Luckily, Gee knew Hillary had a mini-obsession with the family photos, so whenever she saw Hillary, knee deep in outtakes, she'd just smile and pass by. No tricky questions.

At the library, Phoebe was having some difficulty locating the information she needed, since she didn't want to clue in her pal Mrs. Merrihew, the librarian, as to what she was searching for. After a day or two of snooping, Phoebe discovered that Gull Island's town of Eastport Harbor did not issue marriage licenses itself; people seeking to get married had to go onto the mainland and get one from a state bureau. That tidbit redirected her, but not knowing the date of the wedding caused problems; and William Callahan was not an uncommon name in New England. Phoebe was spending a lot of time online and at the microfiche table.

Neeve, meanwhile, was trying to hatch a plan to get her cosmetics bag back from Sloan, and nothing was inspiring her; but she'd come up with something soon. That was for *sure*! Meanwhile, every time she saw Sloan at clinic she wanted to throttle her, but instead she simply glared at her and walked in the other direction. Sloan seemed not to notice, but once Neeve turned around quickly and caught Sloan staring at her and the other cousins as they looped arms and did a pretend cancan line out of the Marina. Sloan had seemed jealous for sure, Neeve had decided.

By Thursday, the walls of the Dorm were all painted, the floor upstairs was waxed; they'd glued burlap to the coffee table and, in an amazing act of compromise on Kate's part, painted it apple green — just the color of Sloan's shorts the night of their sleepover. Even Kate had to admit it looked amazing.

Kate had also borrowed Sheila's sewing machine to run up some plain but spanking white starched sailcloth curtains for all of the windows, and they'd painted the dirty old poles to hang them on. Neeve had the cute idea to paint the poles hot pink, and shockingly enough, Kate had agreed. It turned out to be a great touch. Meanwhile, Kate had had to give in to the ways of the world and submit to having Gee order new white canvas slipcovers for the couch and chairs; without a credit card of her own, it just hadn't been possible. Then they'd painted all of the furniture upstairs in a fresh coat of white, and now, Neeve decided, it was time to add flourishes everywhere. She just had to convince Kate.

Friday afternoon, Hillary came bursting into the Dorm with

a bang. Kate and Neeve were in the middle of a heated discussion about why coating the loft's banister with red glitter was a terrible idea, and they turned, annoyed by the interruption.

Hillary was out of breath; she'd run from the main house.

"What?" asked Neeve brusquely.

Wordlessly, Hillary handed over a photograph. It was Neeve's dad with a young blonde girl sitting on his lap at a beach barbecue. They were both laughing and hoisting bottles of Budweiser beer in the air.

Neeve felt like she'd been socked in the stomach again. She'd never get used to seeing her dad with anyone but her mum.

"Is that the girl?" Hillary asked quietly.

"Yes," answered Neeve. Kate peered over her shoulder to look at the picture.

"Weird," she breathed quietly.

Neeve sat down on the bottom stair and fanned herself with the photo.

"Are you alright?" asked Kate and Hillary simultaneously.

"Yeah." She looked back down at the photo. "It's weird that she was a part of this family and we've never even heard of her." There was another long pause. "She's really pretty. She looks nothing like Mum, though."

Hillary and Kate listened without speaking. Finally, Hillary asked if she could see the picture again. It was passed around and they all three took the time to study it.

"It looks like they were *really* young," said Hillary.

"Yeah," agreed Kate. Then a look of shock crossed her face. "You don't think they got married because . . ."

Neeve felt suddenly protective of her father. She snatched the picture back from Kate. "Because the girl was pregnant? Is that what you're thinking? I highly doubt it," she huffed. But she didn't feel as sure as she sounded. That very thought had been lurking in her mind; what if there were other children? What if she had half-brothers or sisters somewhere that she knew nothing about? Could her dad be so heartless as to never have introduced them? And worse, what if he'd just ditched them altogether? What would that say about him, as a person? Neeve would have to revise her entire opinion of him, this man whom she'd allowed to drag her all over the world! What if he'd been running from something all along? Like a family back in . . . Gull Island? Neeve shuddered. She felt like she might be sick to her stomach.

Hillary took a step closer and put her hand on Neeve's arm. *"Grab the reins, cowgirl,"* she instructed. "Don't let your imagination run wild. Your dad is great and if there was anything really important about this marriage, I'm sure he'd have told you by now." She glared at Kate for emphasis, as if warning her not to bring up any more terrible possibilities.

Neeve nodded and took a deep breath. "Yes. True. Okay, then." She stood up. "I hope Phoebe finds out some real information soon, though. Like today. The suspense is really killing me." She looked at Hillary and knew Hillary was doubting whether she ever should have produced the photo. "Hey, Hilly, thanks. You did the right thing. I needed to see it."

Hillary shrugged. "You're welcome, I guess."

But Neeve knew Hillary wouldn't look for any more photographs. The last thing Hillary would want to do at this moment would be to get Neeve more upset. *Now Kate, on the other hand . . .* , thought Neeve. She spun to face her.

"Okay, state your reasons for *no* glitter, and I'll state mine *for* glitter, and we'll see what Hillary thinks." Neeve stood with her hands on her hips.

Kate sighed. "Neeve, we've been over this and over this . . ."

"You know what?" Hillary held her palms up in the air to face Neeve and Kate. "Please don't get me involved. I hate decorating and I hate girl fights. Just leave me out of it, okay?"

"Fine," huffed Neeve. She had been sure that with Hillary's support they could override Kate. She looked at Kate, who was smirking in victory. *The nerve!*

"Aargh!" Neeve roared. She spun on her heel to return to one of Kate's all-white, mindless little tasks. "If all you care about is making a deadline instead of making a cool house, then there's nothing I can do to save you."

▲

Saturday, the girls had the whole day to work on the Dorm. But naturally, it turned out to be a sparkling blue beach day — clear skies, warm sun, and a very light cool breeze. According to the weather report, the ocean was as flat as a pancake — just the way the girls liked it. So despite Kate's furious pleas, she was outvoted three to one, and they went to the beach for the morning, promising to return home to work after lunch.

Neeve cycled with her boogie board slung over her shoulders, and when they reached the beach, their friend Talbot was there. He had grown up in Jamaica and knew how to surf really well; he also had a crush on Neeve, and offered to teach her how to ride the waves — this being a perfect day for beginners.

So Neeve splashed away the morning riding tiny, slow waves while Phoebe read and Hillary played Kadima and then volleyball with some other kids they'd met through Talbot. Tucker was there, hanging around the counter at The Snack, talking to Gina, and a bunch of other kids from clinic were there, too. Kate sat in a beach chair she'd rented, huffily needle-pointing a pillow for the Dorm. It was clear that this was all just a major waste of time to her.

At lunchtime, the girls went up to The Snack to order, then sat with their trays on the rough wooden benches of a picnic table. Neeve's skin was sticky with salt under her shirt and tight with the beginnings of a sunburn, but she didn't mind. It had been fun learning to ride the waves. Unfortunately, though, Talbot had had to go in to work at Booker's, the sporting goods store in town, and Tucker wasn't leaving his post at the counter, even as the lunch rush started, so the girls were alone.

Just as they were beginning to eat, Sloan and a few members

of her ever-changing posse arrived. Sloan nodded at the Calla-hans, as if she were too busy to talk to them, but they didn't care. No interactions with Sloan ever ended very well. But Lark smiled and said "Hi," and the Callahans responded in kind.

The girls, starved from all the ocean air and activity (Neeve and Hillary, anyway), quickly chowed their club sandwiches and grilled cheeses, and slurped down their frosty fountain Cokes. Then they peeled the paper off the little pieces of Bazooka bubble gum that The Snack gave away with every or-der, and read their comics to each other.

When they stood to leave, Sloan stood as well. They didn't notice her until she was right next to them dumping her tray. The garbage was sticky with old, spilled soda and covered in desperate flies seeking sugar. The flies in Africa were always trying to land in Neeve's eyes to drink her tears and it drove her bonkers; today she waved them away in exasperation.

Out of the blue, Sloan looked directly at Neeve. "So I was asking my mom about those pictures, because I thought I might let you have one or two . . . not all of them, of course, because the trade still isn't complete . . ."

But Neeve waved Sloan off like *she* was a pesky fly and walked around her. "Thanks, anyway, Sloan, but I don't need them anymore," she said breezily, but inside her stomach was doing flip-flops. Oh, how she wanted those pictures! But her tactic worked! Sloan was caught off-guard by her offhandedness; she was used to having the power in these negotiations, not the other way around. Sloan stumbled for something else to add.

"Well, my mom told me all about the wedding, and everything. And about Serena."

Neeve stopped in her tracks, and Sloan smiled a smug and triumphant smile. She knew she'd regained the power.

"Oh, really?" said Neeve casually. She couldn't let on that Sloan knew more than she did, or Sloan would lord it over her and refuse to tell her any more.

"Yeah, she knew her a bit from growing up. The Castells used to come here in the summers."

"Oh, I'd heard that," lied Neeve. She was playing it cool, but inside she was boiling with a mixture of rage and curiosity. So the girl's name was Serena Castell! And Sloan clearly knew now that Serena wasn't Neeve's mother! The others watched Neeve carefully to see what else she'd say. They seemed to know they shouldn't get involved unless they absolutely had to, and for this, Neeve was grateful. She was beginning to figure out how to play Sloan, and if someone else chimed in, it could ruin the whole thing.

Sloan studied Neeve, trying to gauge how much Neeve actually knew. Neeve could practically see the wheels turning in Sloan's devious mind as she worked out what else to reveal. Everyone was still. Finally, Sloan spoke.

"My mom said it was really sad the way it ended. Everyone on Gull was upset." Then she turned on her heel and went back to her group, who'd been watching her the whole time, unable to hear what she was saying.

Neeve was speechless. She wouldn't chase after Sloan to ask

for more information; she still had her dignity, after all. The others looked dumbfounded. Finally, Phoebe found her voice. "Do you want me to go after her and grill her?" She looked eager for a fight.

Neeve turned to look at Phoebe, who had murderous rage in her eyes. Neeve had to laugh.

"No, Bee. Don't give her the satisfaction. Just look at it this way. Now you know the bride's name, too! That should help!" Neeve's voice sounded more confident than she felt. Inside she was shaky and scared. What did it mean that everyone on Gull was upset by the way it had ended? Was her dad a bad guy? Did people hate him? This was starting to sound worse and worse.

"I'm going to the library right now, then!" declared Phoebe. And with that, she marched down to the beach to gather her things.

"Wait! What about the reveal tomorrow?!" Kate called after her uselessly.

As Neeve passed Sloan's table, she caught Lark's eye. From the sympathetic look that Lark was giving her, she could tell that Lark knew Sloan had just been mean to her, and she could tell Lark felt bad. Neeve attempted a smile, and Lark set her jaw and turned her head to glare at Sloan. Then she looked back quickly at Neeve.

"Thanks," mouthed Neeve. *Maybe Lark would become a friend after all,* she thought.

CHAPTER ELEVEN

The Reveal

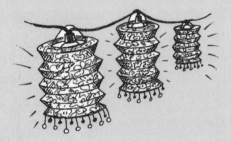

$\mathcal{B}$ack at the Dorm that afternoon, Neeve needed distraction. She threw herself into the redecoration with zeal, beginning four new projects, and quickly tossing off instructions to a willing Hillary and an ever-poutier Kate. Bossy old Neeve was back, and there was nothing to do but follow her directions. Hillary was humoring her because she felt so bad about the scene with Sloan at the beach, and Neeve was making use of Hillary's sympathy.

First she assigned Hillary to tape off a large rectangle on the downstairs wall, then fill it in with blackboard paint. Kate fumed as she watched her newly painted, pristine white wall get slowly covered with the sooty paint. Next, Neeve instructed Kate to push back the furniture and tape off a section of the floor so that they could paint on an area rug. Kate stated that she thought it would look messy and take too long, but one look from Hillary silenced her, and she sulkily began shoving the chairs and couch around.

Neeve, meanwhile, had discovered a cache of Chinese paper lanterns in the garage. She was involved with trying to string them along underneath the loft and figure out if they could somehow be lit. She'd also decided that the lampshades upstairs needed spiffing up, and she wanted to cut up a bunch of grass hula skirts Gee had given them from some old summer luau and glue them around the shades for a tropical look. Kate viewed this project with particular alarm.

"But Neeve, it will look so junky!" she wailed.

Neeve set her mouth in a grim line. Her arms were killing her from trying to secure the lanterns overhead, and she had to admit she herself wasn't sure about the hula skirts. But Kate's attitude was bugging her, and Kate's desperation to meet some stupid self-imposed deadline was driving Neeve wild.

"Come on, Kate!" Neeve said impatiently. "Think outside the box for once! Or don't they teach you how to do that in the American suburbs?"

Kate's temper flared. "Listen, just because you grew up in some wildly cool third-world vacation destination doesn't mean you get to come here and junk this place up to make it look, like, ethnic, or whatever!"

Hillary had been watching the start of the fight in shock. Suddenly she came to her senses. "Guys! Stop! This is crazy!"

Neeve and Kate were both breathing hard and staring daggers at each other, but they were silent.

Hillary stepped closer; Neeve could see even through her anger at Kate that Hillary was unsure of herself. As an only child and a jock who avoided cliquey girls, Hillary was unused to girls fighting. And sure enough, Neeve noticed distractedly, she had to draw on her extensive sports experience now. "Uh, okay. I think we need a cooldown period. Like a timeout. Then, uh, I think we should run home only the projects we've already started, and we can just . . . vote on the other stuff when Phoebe gets back, okay?"

Neeve and Kate took one last hard look at each other, then turned away.

"Okay," they agreed, after a moment. But the bad feelings still hung in the air.

At four-thirty, Gee rang the dinner gong to signal the girls. She had been instructed to stay well away from the Dorm until the reveal, but she needed them to get ready for their usual Saturday night outing to five-fifteen mass at the Cliff Church, and then dinner afterward at Cabot's Clam Shack. But Phoebe still wasn't back from the library yet.

Suspending their fight for the time being, Neeve and Kate, along with Hillary, quickly discussed what they should say to Gee about Phoebe's absence. They knew they'd have to tell the truth about Phoebe's whereabouts; they just didn't want to tell Gee *why* Phoebe was there. Finally, they decided to say as little as possible and leave it at that.

They quickly showered and dressed in slightly dressy outfits — Neeve in an embroidered off-the-shoulder blouse from India and an eccentric batik sarong she'd wrapped around herself as a skirt, and the others in varying degrees of sporty preppiness. They arrived at church just in time to secure the last seats in the back row, where Gee liked to sit (Gee always said the front row was for sinners and show-offs, which cracked Neeve up). Gee had been surprised that Phoebe wasn't with the others, but not mad; Phoebe was so responsible that Gee knew there must be a good reason for her absence. She'd left instructions with Sheila that if Phoebe turned up, she could ride her bike to meet them. That seemed to be her penance for being late.

And sure enough, about twenty-five minutes into the mass, something caught Neeve's eye in the doorway. It was a freshly showered Phoebe, in a long, pale blue cotton sundress, and she was craning her head to see where Gee and the cousins were. Neeve couldn't raise her hand to wave, but Phoebe quickly caught sight of them and realized she'd never fit into the jammed pew, so she settled for standing in the doorway to the equally crammed back porch. Neeve looked again and Phoebe caught her eye this time. Neeve raised her eyebrows and Phoebe gave a small but emphatic nod.

Shocked, Neeve turned back to face the altar. So Phoebe had found something. But was this good or bad? Suddenly Neeve wasn't sure she wanted to know all the details. If it was bad, it could change her relationship with her dad forever.

The agony of sitting through mass while Phoebe had the information just twenty-five feet away was excruciating for Neeve. So when she went up for communion, she didn't return to her seat but instead made for the back porch and waved to Phoebe to accompany her.

Outside, they sat on the lowest step and tried to peel the cement-like communion wafers from the roofs of their mouths so they could talk. It took a minute. Finally, Neeve whispered, "So?"

Phoebe looked at her, clear blue eyes met clear blue eyes, as in a mirror, and Phoebe said, "I found it. Their wedding announcement. In the *Boston Globe.*"

Neeve closed her eyes for a moment. As if the photos hadn't been proof enough, the existence of a major newspaper article covering the event sealed it. It was true. It had really happened.

She opened her eyes. "And?" She had to know more.

Phoebe looked at her sympathetically. "I made a printout of the article, but I had to leave it at Gee's. I couldn't really bring it here, you know?" She shrugged and gestured to the church behind them.

Neeve sighed and put her hand over her eyes, as if to shade them. "Just tell me what you remember then."

But the mass was ending. They had to stand up from the steps to let people out, and as they stepped to the side to resume their conversation, the others came bounding out of the church, with Gee following them at a more dignified but still lively pace.

Hillary's and Kate's faces were both full of questions — their raised eyebrows asking silently if Phoebe had found something. Phoebe nodded slightly at them, but no further information was forthcoming, as Gee was upon them.

"Hello, my little heathen," she said, kissing Phoebe on the cheek. "What happened to you?"

Luckily, Phoebe had done other reading at the library, so as she described it to Gee on their way to the car, the other three dropped back.

"So?" asked Hillary quietly. Kate leaned in toward Neeve to hear the reply.

"She found a wedding announcement in the *Globe*. But that's as far as we got." Neeve was distracted and disappointed. It crossed her mind to fake being sick so she could go home now and read the article, but it would really be a hassle for Gee and the others to drive her all the way home and then have to come back over here for dinner. Plus, she had to admit, she loved the lobster stew at Cabot's so much that she couldn't have to wait another week to have it. *That article isn't going anywhere, silly,* she told herself sternly. *You'll just have to wait.*

"Read it out loud!" said Kate eagerly. Hillary flashed her a strange look, as if wondering why Kate sounded so excited. Kate realized her mistake and ducked her head in embarrassment.

The four cousins were sitting on the floor of the loft, where they'd rushed after returning from Cabot's. Phoebe had wordlessly handed the folded article to Neeve, who'd winced as she'd looked at the beautiful studio portrait of the young bride in her lace mantilla.

Neeve complied with Kate's command and began by reading the headline. "'William Francis Callahan and Serena Louise Castell. Transportation heir weds bottling heiress.'"

"Ooh! An heir and an heiress! Fancy!" Kate smiled in anticipation and wiggled in place, and then, seeing the looks on Hillary's and Phoebe's faces, regained her composure and made her face serious again.

"I don't know why they call him an 'heir,'" mumbled Neeve under her breath. "It's kind of a strong word for what you get when you're one of nine."

"Transportation and bottling?" said Phoebe wryly. "Don't drink and drive!" She was trying to lighten the moment and Neeve flashed her a grateful look and resumed reading, but silently this time.

"Out loud!" said Kate again.

But Neeve didn't want to, so she scanned the article and quietly murmured the highlights.

"'June 21, 1984 . . . At Gull Island's Cliff Church . . . presided over by Father Brendan Mulcahy, an uncle of the bride . . . carried a bouquet of peonies and lilacs . . . ten bridesmaids . . . honeymoon in Bermuda . . . to live on Beacon Hill in Boston. . . .'"

When she finished, they all sat in silence, unmoving, unsure of what to do or say next. Then Phoebe, of all people, came and put her arm awkwardly around Neeve's shoulder. "I'm sorry," Phoebe whispered.

Neeve wasn't sure if Phoebe was saying she was sorry it had happened or sorry she'd found the article or what, but the fact of Phoebe being so outwardly sympathetic and affectionate suddenly made her dissolve. Tears seeped from the corners of her eyes and her chest heaved. Phoebe patted her back stiffly, and Kate moved to Neeve's side, murmuring comforting things.

"It's just so weird," said Neeve, trying to pull herself together.

"We know," said Phoebe.

They let her weep quietly for a moment, then Hillary cleared her throat dramatically. Everyone looked up.

"No one's dead," she said.

The others looked at her in confusion, and she continued. "I mean, we're sitting here like we're in mourning, but it's not like Neeve's dad died or anything. He's just been married before. It happens all the time." She shrugged.

Neeve looked up. Suddenly, she felt guilty. Earlier in the summer, Neeve had said almost these exact words to Hillary about her parents' divorce when Hillary was feeling down about the split. No one's dead. It's just different now. Buck up, kiddo.

Neeve took a deep breath. She realized what Hillary was getting at, and she was ashamed of herself for wallowing in self-pity, all because her dad had loved someone else before he loved her mum. She cleared her throat. "You're right," she said. "No one's dead."

Phoebe and Kate eased back from their comforting positions and looked at Neeve, waiting for her to make the next move. Neeve squared her shoulders and sat upright. "And we have a reveal to do tomorrow."

Kate flashed her a look of gratitude, and Neeve smiled. It was time to get back to work.

By ten-thirty that night, Gee was knocking on the door to the Dorm, asking about bedtime. The girls tumbled out, covered in various kinds of glue, paint, and sparkles, and barred the door. They'd made some progress over the past two hours, but now it was like the Dorm was less ready for the reveal than ever: half-finished projects lay everywhere, and there was no end in sight. Kate was working like a dog, frustrated by how far they were from the end. She and Neeve were sniping at each other around every corner, and Phoebe and Hillary were working hard to keep the peace. But Gee didn't see any of that.

"My, you remind me of the mice in *Cinderella,* as they were getting her ready for the ball," Gee laughed. "But I do think it's time for bed, chickadees. You have all day tomorrow — and as long as you like, really. It doesn't have to be tomorrow."

"Yes, it does," said Kate fervently. "We need to move in, too. Summer's flying by!"

Neeve rolled her eyes.

"Well, whatever you like, but I still think you need to get some sleep. It won't be any fun tomorrow if you're overtired. So come along, now. Finish the essentials for tonight and you can come back bright and early in the morning."

The girls ducked back inside to clean up a bit, and Gee called after them that she'd see them up in the big house in fifteen minutes.

Kate began grumpily slamming things around: lids back on paint cans, trays and rollers into the sink upstairs, empty boxes in a pile. The others exchanged looks, and Hillary sighed and whispered, "I'll handle it."

"Kate? What's wrong? Can we help you?"

Kate wheeled around, as if she'd just been waiting for someone to ask. Her blue eyes, usually so mild and friendly, flashed with anger.

"I'll tell you what's wrong. Our whole decorating project is a disaster! And it's taking forever! I don't know why we couldn't have just done it simply, but no, Miss Smarty Pants, Miss I'm-Better-Than-Everyone-and-My-Dramas-and-Ideas-Come-First had to take over, as usual!" Kate was choking back tears.

Neeve was shocked. Obviously she'd known that she and Kate were having tension, but this was crazy! "Kate . . . ," she said.

Kate wheeled around to face her. "It's true! You're ruining everything!"

Neeve gasped. But then her own anger flared right up. "Listen, I can't help it that this thing with my dad came up, and it's not like it's exactly good news. I can't imagine the floods of tears we'd be having every day if it was your perfect suburban dad who'd been married before, your perfect little suburban family we were talking about. And as for the whole stupid decorating project, I'm sorry that I'm ruining it for you! I just didn't think that creating a white box to live in was that much of an achievement. But if that's what you still want, we'll just bag all the other stuff. See if I care!" And she stormed out.

As she ran up the hill to the main house, Neeve's heart was pounding with fury, but also with shock at the things she'd just said. *Well, tough!* she thought. Kate had been pecking at her for weeks now, and it was her problem if she was mad, not Neeve's. Neeve was just trying to help. She wanted the Dorm to be cool.

She darted around to the side entrance so she wouldn't have to pass Gee in the kitchen and explain anything. Upstairs, her annoyance grew as she realized she'd either have to stay in the room she shared with Kate, or make a huge statement by going to sleep in one of the many guest rooms. She huffed in exasperation, and decided she'd just put on her pj's, get in bed, turn out the light, and pretend to be asleep when Kate came in.

Lying in bed a few moments later, the adrenaline from the fight began to wear off, and a wisp of guilt crept in, slow and sneaky, like the island's evening fog. *Maybe Kate's right,* thought Neeve. *Maybe I should have just let her have her way with the Dorm. What difference would it have made? Why did I have to take over? Why do I always have to be in control of everything?*

And the thing with her dad, too. She had to admit it had

kind of taken over her life, and the others', to a degree, too. Neeve rubbed her eyes, but then a flash of annoyance swept over her again. It wasn't like Kate had ever gone to the attic to look for any of the stuff about her dad, anyway! She wasn't spending any of her own time or energy on it. And Kate had really seemed into the gory details tonight when they were reading the wedding announcement! Like she was enjoying it! It was kind of creepy, actually, now that Neeve thought about it.

The bedroom door opened and then closed, and Neeve clamped her eyes shut and tried to even out her breathing. Without a word, Kate moved across the room to her bed, and there was some rustling as she must've been changing. Then she climbed into her bed. They were both silent.

But then, "Neeve?"

"Hillary?"

"Yeah. Kate's sleeping in my room."

"Good!" said Neeve, flouncing up onto her elbow so she was facing Hillary.

"Neeve . . ."

"She's being a total brat!" said Neeve, all riled up again. She sat up and clicked on the light. Hillary squinted and propped herself up on one elbow.

"Well, she was, just now, but you have to see her side of it . . ."

"There is no side!" Neeve was furious. "There's just one side, and it's this: we're family. We're all supposed to be on the same team. If one of us is in trouble, the others help! And as for that dumb Dorm, I told her she can do it her way. *Whatever!* Who cares if we're living in an igloo, all white everywhere, for the rest of the summer!"

Hillary burst out laughing. "An igloo! That's good!"

Neeve cracked a smile. "It's like the stupid old North Pole in there!"

They got laughing, and the laughter felt good. They stretched it out by adding on other silly stuff about vanilla ice cream and Frosty the Snowman.

Suddenly, the door opened, and there was Phoebe.

"What's going on in here?" she asked. "We could hear you laughing in the other room, even with both doors closed!"

Neeve sighed a big after-laugh sigh. "Nothing. Hillary was just making me feel better."

Then Kate appeared in the doorway and Neeve's smile faded. Kate had a nervous look on her face, but she came into the room anyway.

"Neeve . . . ," she began.

"What?" said Neeve huffily.

"I'm sorry, really I am." Kate rushed to Neeve's side, climbing up onto her bed, next to her.

"Humph," said Neeve, milking the apology for all it was worth. She didn't think she was quite as mad right now as she'd been before.

"It's just that, sometimes, well, you know . . . ," Kate began lamely.

"I know what? That you're obsessed with the Dorm and

greedy about getting to have all the ideas?" As it turned out, Neeve couldn't let everything go. Not yet.

Kate's eyes flashed with rekindled anger.

"Guys . . . ," interrupted Phoebe. They turned to look at her, and she shut the door behind her and came to sit on the bed, too.

"Listen," Phoebe continued. "You need to settle this once and for all. Hillary and I can't stand all the bickering. You're starting to ruin our summer. It's serious now. So you need to just work out this acrimony. Right now."

Neeve and Kate looked away from Phoebe and stared daggers at each other. Finally, Kate spoke up.

"I don't know what acrimony means, but I'm just sick of everything being about Neeve all the time," she said.

"It's not like I can help it!" said Neeve indignantly. "I didn't want to discover this new information about my dad!"

"Besides that, all the decorating stuff, it always has to be your way," continued Kate.

"Well I think you're totally uptight and conservative!" spat Neeve.

"I think you try too hard to be different and creative!" Kate replied.

Neeve exploded. "I *am* different! I don't live some white-bread boring life where nothing ever changes. I travel the world. I meet new people and I get to try new things. And I like it!"

"You think you're so cool, Neeve! You're such a know-it-all. Everything has to be your special way or it's just 'American,' or 'boring'! Well I am an American, and I like it here. So why don't you just go back to your super-cool worldly life in whatever god-forsaken place you call home this week!" Kate's cheeks were bright red and her breath was coming in fast, furious gasps.

Neeve felt stung, as if she'd been slapped. Her mouth hung open for a minute and then it was all too much for her. She hung her head and began to cry in huge, gulping sobs. Phoebe patted her back awkwardly while she cried, and the others were silent. Finally, she took a deep, ragged breath and found her voice again.

"I don't call *any* place home! I don't *have* a home! I don't even know if I have a *family* anymore!" Neeve was hiccuping now and she didn't care. "I just wanted the Dorm to be my home for real, forever. That's why I wanted it to be good. So we can always come back there and be together, and it will be cool and homey, and just for us! And maybe I *am* jealous of you and your life. You've had the same house always, and the same best friends, and you've gone to the same school since kindergarten, and your mom and dad are totally normal and American and they don't have accents like my mum, and that's just *grand*. It's all just so easy for you! But all I have are the things I've picked up along the way: whatever fits in my bags and a couple of pen pals." Neeve covered her eyes with her hands. She was overwhelmed with self-pity, but she was also relieved by her confession.

Kate looked shocked. She didn't know what to say at first. Finally, she took a deep breath. "Look, Neeve. My life *is* totally boring and white-bread, as you say. But I'm good at it. I know the ropes, I know the rules. If I had to pick up and move to some foreign country, I'd be finished. I could never survive, let alone make friends and pick up cool local customs and stylish stuff like you do. I didn't realize it was so hard for you, because I feel like you're always throwing it in our faces that we're these losers who've never been anywhere exotic or lived any adventures, and after a while, it's annoying. Your life *is* so exciting, and mine *is* so dull, and I just get tired of you rubbing it in all the time." She folded her hands in her lap and shrugged. "I'm sorry. I had no idea it was so hard for you." She laughed a little. "You hide it so well!"

Neeve took her face out from behind her hands. "Well, I have to. I need to be a happy camper or my parents will get upset. You know my dad's motto: *Callahans don't cry.*" She winced as she said it; she'd never realized how bad it sounded before.

"But don't they know how hard it is for you?" asked Kate in concern.

"Yeah, kind of." Neeve waved her hand dismissively. "But you know, if you pretend to like something for long enough, you start to think you actually do. And then it's pretty easy to convince other people that you like it, too." She smiled a feeble smile, and it was her turn to shrug.

Kate reached over and put her warm, competent hand on top of Neeve's tiny, cold one. "Maybe you should tell them you don't want to move anymore," she said, in a low, comforting voice. Now that Neeve's defenses were down and it was clear that she needed help, Kate was back to her mothering role. But somehow, this time, Neeve found it soothing instead of annoying.

"Maybe . . ." Neeve wasn't sure, and she couldn't decide right now. "I just don't know what to think about them anymore. I wouldn't even know what to say. Like, *'Hi, it's me. I know you were married before and, by the way, I never want to move again, okay?'* And anyway, then I'm stuck in Singapore forever, and they don't even let you chew gum in public there!"

Hillary, who'd been listening in silence from the other bed, laughed out loud. "Wow! They'd have a field day with The Snack there, giving out all that Bazooka!"

This broke the tension and everyone laughed, even Neeve.

"Look, I'm sorry, Neeve. I had no idea about all of this. I just thought you were trying to be a princessy control-freak." Kate looked as if she might cry herself, now.

Neeve laughed again. "I was that, too! But I'm sorry about messing up all of your neat plans. We can do the Dorm your way. It's okay —"

"I know!" interrupted Phoebe, holding one finger in the air. "What about if we give you each an official title and role in the redecorating process?" Everyone looked at her skeptically. "Like, what if Kate is the chief contractor and decorator, and Neeve is the stylist and accessorizer?"

"Well what does that accomplish?" asked Neeve. She wasn't sure they needed titles this late in the game.

"It means Kate does all the big changes and painting and all that, and hands out the jobs. But when all the technical stuff is done, she has to back off, and Neeve, you get to take over and arrange things any way you like — adding or subtracting props and stuff like that."

"So I'm basically done, then, right?" asked Kate skeptically.

"Yes," agreed Phoebe. "And you can't interfere with anything Neeve moves around, or puts in there. However you, Neeve, can't start any more projects involving glue, or paint, or anything. We just finish up what's started and move on."

"And we move the reveal to next Sunday," added Hillary with a defiant look on her face.

Kate and Neeve looked at the others and then back at each other again. It sounded as if they were each gaining something and losing something in the bargain, but at least it was fair and the fighting could stop. Also it would allow them to wrap things up in a leisurely and friendly fashion.

"Okay by me," Neeve agreed, reaching out slowly to shake Kate's hand.

Kate smiled and took Neeve's hand. Neeve, suddenly inspired, remembered their special cousins' handshake from years earlier, and she quickly changed their grip and twisted her hand from side to side to cement the deal. Kate laughed. "I can't believe you remembered that!" and she did it back to Neeve. It was settled.

"Cousins forever," whispered Neeve, as she grabbed Kate in a hug.

"Cousins forever," Kate whispered back.

CHAPTER TWELVE

Party On

*M*onday morning at breakfast, Gee dropped a bombshell.

"I've been thinking you girls ought to ask Sloan here for a sleepover," she began, reading glasses perched low on her nose so she could peer over them at the foursome.

Neeve nearly choked on her black coffee, and the others looked at Gee in alarm.

"Why?" asked Neeve, when she had recovered.

"To return the hospitality. She was awfully nice to have all four of you over, and when I saw her mother at the church rummage sale last week, she told me that Sloan hasn't stopped talking about it since."

"I'll bet," muttered Phoebe.

"Hmmm?" asked Gee.

"Nothing," said Neeve, glaring at Phoebe. The last thing she wanted was for the whole makeup trade thing to come up. Then she'd wind up having to tell Gee everything.

"Sloan's so mean, though," said Kate.

"We're really not crazy about her, Gee," said Hillary. "And what would we even do with her?" she continued, turning to the others.

"You could have a little picnic supper here for a group of friends first, if that would make it easier. Then Sloan could just sleep over afterward," suggested Gee with a twinkle in her eye. She'd clearly had that part of the plan up her sleeve the whole time.

"Yes!" said Neeve enthusiastically. She loved having people over and had been starting to miss her usual role of hostess. "We could have Talbot, and Tucker, and Marley, and . . . maybe even Lark."

"Oh, she does seem nice, actually." Kate was getting into it now, too, Neeve noted with pleasure.

And so it was settled. Friday night, they'd have a picnic dinner with fried chicken, potato salad, and coleslaw. And for dessert, watermelon and make-your-own sundaes. Neeve could hardly wait.

At clinic that morning, the wind was blowing strong, so the instructors wasted no time in hurrying them all out on their little boats. Neeve had no time to invite anyone to Friday's party before clinic started. But all through their lessons, with the wind whipping her hair around and pushing into her lungs in enormous gusts, Neeve looked forward to issuing the invitations. Her excitement had made her feel expansive and generous; she'd even temporarily forgotten her dislike for Sloan.

When they were finally sprung at twelve o'clock, Neeve invited a few kids she liked from clinic, and Tucker, too. Everyone was excited and agreed to come, and Neeve was floating on air, she was so happy. Finally, she bounded over to Sloan.

"Hi!" she said breathlessly. "Want to come over Friday night for dinner and a sleepover?"

Sloan looked at her coolly, then bent her head to inspect her manicure, which was flawless. "I might have a date that night." She looked up to gauge Neeve's reaction, but Neeve willed her features to look unimpressed. The last thing she needed was for Sloan to think she thought she was cool. Neeve didn't flinch, but waited patiently.

"But I'll see if I can put him off," said Sloan slowly. "It's always a good idea to make them wait," she added knowledgeably.

"Yeah," agreed Neeve, who knew there was no such "him" or date. "So six o'clock Friday then. And bring your bathing suit!" she said. "And my makeup or photos," she added bravely as she galloped over to meet up with the others.

▲

The girls had decided that they should sleep in the Dorm on Friday night, since that way they could all be in one room together, and no twosome would be stuck alone with Sloan in their room. So after clinic each day that week, they worked on finishing up their various projects and making the Dorm livable, if not totally reveal-worthy, by Friday.

Neeve was also obsessed with the party. She wanted it to be a blast, and when she wasn't busy inviting people, she was occupied with cooking up all kinds of activities to keep everyone amused. She stopped by the Little Store, the tiny beach-oriented general store near Gee's house, and bought sparklers from their friend Farren, the owner. She had Hillary help her lug the ancient but functional croquet set out of the garage, then hose it down and set it up on a level section of the side lawn. They raked and hosed off the neglected trampoline, and blew up some rafts that Gee brought home for them. And they made sure to accompany Sheila to buy the dinner supplies, just to make sure they got every possible sundae topping they could think of.

At first, all of this activity helped to keep her mind off the subject of her father's first marriage. When Phoebe had brought home the clipping from the newspaper, Neeve had been overwhelmed by the reality of it all. She'd folded the article into a tiny square and tucked it away, with the photo Hillary had found, in her bedside table. And all week, she hadn't been tempted to look at them again. *Maybe I'm just better off not knowing for now,* she'd thought. *Maybe he'll tell me when the time is right.* But after a few days of peace, she was pulled right back into the drama again.

The girls had gone to town on Friday after clinic to pick up a few last-minute supplies — a volleyball for the pool (which had a net they'd set up but no ball), a tub of homemade hot fudge sauce from The Dip, and some guacamole from Callie's Cupboard — and Neeve was off on her own at the drugstore, buying bug spray for the evening and some shampoo that she needed.

She was standing in the aisle at White's Drugstore, with its low shelves, trying to decide between the Apple Cider Clarifying Shampoo or the Piña Colada Moisturizing Shampoo (she had a hard time knowing if her hair needed clarifying or moisturizing, just like she could never decide if her face was triangular or heart-shaped when she looked at those makeup tips in *CosmoGIRL*). As she spaced out and tried to decide, her attention drifted to a conversation at the nearby pharmacy counter.

"I thought that was you!" a woman was saying with obvious pleasure.

"How nice to see you!" said another woman. "How have you been?"

"We've been well. Business is great, especially now that summer is here, and everyone's well." Then the woman's voice took on a more concerned tone. "How are *you* all doing these days?"

Some hint of drama in the woman's voice made Neeve turn to see who was speaking. It was the pharmacist, leaning halfway across the counter, looking with great concern at her customer.

The customer was clearly used to the question, and had an upbeat answer. "We're doing fine, really. Of course it's painful to be back here, but we are happy to be home again."

Neeve, shamelessly interested now, studied the woman. She was about Gee's age, a little bit round, but in a pleasant way, with a frosted blond bob, and a peaches-and-cream complexion. Very pretty, and friendly-looking. The expression "well-to-do" popped into Neeve's head. Neeve felt bad for the woman. She seemed nice, and it was clear from their conversation that something bad had happened to her.

"Well, it was just heart-breaking that things had to end that way," said the pharmacist.

"I know," agreed the customer. "I feel the same way. It was just so sad."

Shut up! Neeve yelled at the pharmacist in her mind. *You're making this poor woman feel worse, not better!* She wanted to go and put her arm around the woman and offer her a nice cup of cocoa, the way Gee did when they were sad, but of course, she couldn't.

"So, I'd better be on my way," said the customer brightly. "I've got some grandchildren outside waiting in the car for me!"

"Of course. Well it was sure nice to see you, Mrs. Castell. Send my love to your family!" said the pharmacist.

Mrs. Castell! Neeve dropped the Apple Cider Clarifying Shampoo on the floor and ducked to retrieve it just as Mrs. Castell passed her.

"Pardon me," said the woman kindly, but Neeve didn't dare look up.

"Sorry," Neeve murmured, for more reasons than one.

Back home that afternoon, Neeve was in a funk: mortified, ashamed, and horrified. She replayed the conversation from the drugstore over and over in her mind to see if she could guess what the tragedy was. She had no doubt that it had to do with Serena; Sloan had already told her that things had ended badly. Could it have been that her dad was so mean to Serena that the whole island knew about it? *What if he had hurt her in some way?* Neeve thought in horror at one point (conveniently forgetting that her father was so gentle he wouldn't even kill the giant dung beetles that had crept into their house at night in Kenya and sent the maids screaming to the far recesses of the kitchen).

And then, Mrs. Castell had mentioned grandchildren. Could they be her father's children? Was it possible? Neeve was back in the middle of it all, with no answers in sight. Unless she came clean to Gee. Which she wouldn't. She felt sick at the thought of having Gee explain the horrible particulars of it all to her.

The others were puzzled by Neeve's sudden mood change; she could tell. But she couldn't bring herself to relay what she'd heard. Everything was just making her dad look worse and worse. Neeve fought back tears as the girls straightened up the Dorm for Sloan's arrival. *Callahans don't cry,* she told herself, over and over again. *Callahans don't cry.*

Her mind whirled, but the party setup did much to distract her. After all, socializing was her life!

"Okay, let's have cold drinks and appetizers here," she instructed, gesturing to a side table on the patio. "And then we'll put the buffet there. And dessert . . ." She put her hands on her hips and spun in a slow circle.

"Whatever you say, bossy boots!" said Kate brightly. She kept trying to tease Neeve out of her funk, and Neeve was grateful but not really receptive.

"What are you going to wear?" asked Hillary with some semblance of enthusiasm.

Neeve laughed in her face. She knew Hillary couldn't care less about clothes, and it was pathetic the way she was trying to fake it. Hillary laughed back, knowing she was busted.

"Sorry," she said. "I just thought it might make you smile!"

"It worked," said Neeve wryly.

"So come on, what's wrong, Neeve?" asked Phoebe. "Is it something to do with your dad? Or has some new calamity befallen you and you're afraid to confess it to us?"

"What did Phoebe just say?" whispered Kate to Hillary.

"Beats me," replied Hillary with a shrug. "I'm only twelve."

Neeve laughed again. "Did you just turn to a new page in your vocabulary workbook today, Bee?"

Phoebe looked miffed, but Hillary clapped. "'Atta girl! That's our Neeve!" she hooted. Neeve curtseyed. Nothing like doling out some teasing to make her feel better.

"Hey, why did we never think to call you 'Spelling Bee'?"

wondered Neeve aloud, tapping her finger against her lips in fake deep thought.

"Alright, fine. That's what I get for being nice. For being a concerned cousin," said Phoebe in a long-suffering voice. But Neeve could tell she wasn't really mad. "So are you going to tell us or not?" demanded Phoebe.

"Not," said Neeve. "For now," she added in a gentler tone.

"Okay, but then no more moping," said Phoebe, imitating Neeve's bossiest voice.

"Fine," agreed Neeve. And she did have to admit she felt better already.

By six-thirty everyone had arrived except Sloan, and the party was in full swing. Even Lark had come and had greeted the cousins warmly, and that made Neeve especially happy. She'd had a good vibe about Lark from the beginning, and she was pleased to see that her social radar still worked.

Upon their arrival, Gee had welcomed each guest. Then she'd gone off to sit in the kitchen, stating that she didn't want to hover. Tucker, who could attend the party only briefly, went and talked with Gee and Sheila in the kitchen for a while, just adding fuel to the fire of their love for him, teased Neeve. (Tucker had been to the house a couple of times already this summer and the girls laughingly debated whether it was his insatiable appetite or his old-fashioned manners that made Gee and Sheila worship him.)

In her role as hostess, Neeve was in her glory. She had chosen her outfit of green raw silk harem pants and a fitted black halter top very carefully, wanting to be sure she was neither too dressy nor too casual. She also wanted to be able to play croquet or jump on the tramp if she was so inclined. Her elaborate hairdo of pinned-up knots looked wonderful but made pool games out of the question, so she just floated around the party instead, sharing sparkling conversation with their fifteen-or-so guests, whacking a few croquet balls when it was her turn, and hiking up her pants before flawlessly executing her best trampoline trick: a back flip that looked much harder and scarier than it was.

It wasn't until Sheila brought out all the bowls and platters of food that Sloan finally arrived with her overnight bag. Neeve crossed the terrace to greet her, and heard Gee asking for Sloan's parents, quick with a cute anecdote about one of the many times Sloan's father had been at their house for dinner. Neeve was proud of Gee's warmth, despite the fact that Sloan didn't deserve it. It was so great to have a grandmother who was interested in making your friends comfortable, she thought. *That must be where my dad gets it,* her brain automatically added. Neeve was frowning at the thought of her father just as Sloan turned to say hello.

"Oh, you're mad I'm late," said Sloan without a trace of sorrow in her voice.

"Actually, I didn't really . . ." Neeve was stuck. She couldn't say she didn't care or hadn't noticed without sounding like a really bad hostess. She narrowed her eyes. Was Sloan setting her up to say something mean? She couldn't tell. "I'm just glad you're here," she said finally.

"Yeah, me too," said Sloan, scanning the crowd. "Where should I put my bag?"

"Oh, sorry," said Neeve, instantly remorseful that she hadn't offered to do something with it first, then quickly annoyed at herself for apologizing to Sloan within her first two minutes there. *How does Sloan always seem to nab the upper hand in every exchange?* wondered Neeve distractedly. They stuck Sloan's bag back in the kitchen and went to join the line at the buffet, where the food was already being rapidly depleted by the hungry partyers.

After dinner, pretty much everyone went into the pool. Sloan rummaged through her suitcase for her bathing suit and changed in the powder room in the big house, and Neeve gave up on trying to look great and changed too. They played volleyball, Marco Polo, and Shark for over an hour. When the sun began to drop down in the west, the air grew cool and people got out. Neeve instigated a watermelon seed-spitting contest that was vicious and fun, and sent more than a few people back into the pool. And then they did the sundaes, creating gobby confections of fudge and marshmallow studded with Reese's Pieces and M&M's.

As they finished dessert, a few parents showed up to pick up some of the guests, and the others, who had ridden bikes, began to leave. Neeve was dreading the time when they'd be alone with Sloan; she hadn't planned any activities for that part of the evening, and she couldn't imagine just sitting around and talking with Sloan all night.

By nine o'clock, it was just the Callahans and Sloan, helping Sheila and Gee to clean up, and Neeve didn't want it to end. Besides the fact that cleaning up with Gee was always fun (she'd turn the music up loud on the boom box in the kitchen and they'd all dance and sing), the time was drawing near for them to go down to the Dorm, just the cousins and Sloan.

As they finished up, Neeve studied Sloan's interaction with Sheila out of the corner of her eye. Sloan was the son of Sheila's half-brother, so Sheila was sort of Sloan's half-aunt. Only the two parts of the family were not on good terms. Sloan and Sheila seemed to more or less ignore each other, except when direct interaction was necessary; then, a frosty politeness took over. As Neeve dried a blue and white platter, she thought about how sad it was that Sloan's grandfather had moved to Gull all the way from Ireland, only to have his family split into warring factions just one generation later. *Families need to stick together. Especially in new places!* thought Neeve. Her dad's voice echoed in her head with the phrases she'd heard dozens of times. *Loyalty is everything!* But then anger rose inside of her. *Well, it wasn't exactly loyal of my dad to be married before!* She knew she was being irrational, but she didn't care. She glanced at Sloan; had Sloan brought those pictures she owed Neeve, once and for all? Or the makeup?

"What now?" asked Hillary, interrupting Neeve's train of thought.

"Let's go down to the Dorm," Neeve said decisively, as she stowed the platter in its cupboard. She needed to know what Sloan had brought.

They said goodnight and thank you to Gee and Sheila. And then Sloan grabbed her open, bulging suitcase and they trooped out the back door and across the patio, Gee waving to them from the stoop. Just as they were stepping onto the grass below, Gee called, "Yoo hoo! Neeve! You forgot something!"

Neeve turned and jogged back across the two terrace levels and up to the door. Gee was holding out a small white shopping bag.

"Sheila said this was in the mudroom, dear," said Gee, handing it over.

The bag said simply NEEVE in blue marker on the outside. Neeve peered inside, and there was her makeup bag! Sloan must've brought it along and then forgotten it when they were heading down to the Dorm.

Neeve looked up at Gee and beamed. "Cool!" she said. "Thanks!" And she skipped away to catch up with the others.

CHAPTER THIRTEEN

Stonehenge?

$\mathscr{A}$s Neeve opened the door to the Dorm, Sloan was saying, "Wow! I can't believe your grandmother let you do this! It's amazing!" Sloan's green eyes were wide with admiration. "And it is *so* cool that you get to stay down here by yourselves!"

For the first time, Neeve actually liked Sloan. She was thrilled to have her makeup back, and happy that Sloan recognized the effort they'd put into the redecoration. She was proud of herself and the cousins for the work they'd done, and also proud of Gee that she had trusted them.

"Thanks, Sloan!" called Neeve, swinging the bag in the air.

Sloan looked at her blankly. "For what?"

Neeve was caught off-guard. "Uh . . ." Hadn't Sloan brought the bag?

"What's that?" asked Kate curiously, eyeing the bag. Everyone, including Sloan, looked at Neeve expectantly.

"Oh . . ." Neeve thought fast. "I guess Tucker dropped it

off earlier. It's from . . . Mrs. Hagan — my, uh, visor I left at clinic last week." Everyone seemed satisfied with the answer, and turned back to what they'd been doing. Neeve stood on her toes and hung the bag on a high peg on the wall. She knew no one would bother to look inside of it before she'd had time to explain it in private. Then Neeve plopped down on the couch, completely puzzled. If Sloan hadn't brought it, then who had? Her warm and fuzzy feelings for Sloan quickly faded.

Meanwhile, Sloan climbed the ladder to the loft and plopped her suitcase next to the air mattress the girls had lugged up there earlier. Kate had made the bed with cute gingham sheets, and it had looked so pretty and snug that Neeve herself had wanted to lie right down in it and take a nap.

"Hey!" called Sloan from upstairs. "Let's go explore that hill over there!"

The cousins looked at each other in confusion. "What, now?" Neeve called back up to her, still distracted by the makeup.

Sloan came back down the ladder. "Yeah. Why not? It would be fun."

"But it's so dark out there!" Kate shuddered.

"What would be the point?" asked Phoebe.

"Just for the thrill of it," said Sloan. "Don't you have flash-lights? Or are you chicken?" pressed Sloan.

Neeve drew herself up to her full height, which was far from impressive but would have to do. "No, we're not chicken. It's just that there's nothing to see or do up there. Why don't we just stay here and play a game or something?"

"That's not what I've heard . . . ," Sloan insinuated.

"Why? What have you heard?" Neeve was furious now. *Sloan couldn't possibly know anything about The Sound that we don't already know. Could she?* Sloan was smirking in a totally annoying way.

But Hillary jumped in before Sloan could answer Neeve. "Hey, we never did the sparklers!" she cried indignantly.

"You're right!" agreed Neeve. "Okay then." She turned to Sloan. "Fine. Let's get the sparklers and we can take them up on the hill." Whatever Sloan knew, or thought she knew, Neeve needed to find out. Now. Because it was obvious that Sloan wasn't going to just tell them.

Phoebe sighed heavily and muttered to herself. "If it's not one thing, it's another. Why do I let myself be dragged along in these juvenile schemes? I'll never know . . ." But Neeve noted with a smile that Phoebe was already putting her shoes back on as she said this.

However, there was no budging Kate. As everyone got ready, she sat on the couch and picked up her needlepoint. "I'm not going," she announced.

And there was no convincing her. She argued that she was tired, she had no interest in the plan, she needed to work on her needlepoint, they already had four of them going up the hill, and yes, in fact, she *was* scared of wandering around the woods in the dark, so there.

So Neeve, Phoebe, Hillary, and Sloan set off with their

flashlights, sparklers, and a small book of matches from Cabot's Clam Shack. Neeve was filled with so many feelings — anger, confusion, fear — that she couldn't even speak. She just let Sloan lead the way, and she followed.

▲

It was dark, but not pitch black, because the outdoor lights from Gee's house cast illumination to the far corners of the yard. But as they left the immediate vicinity of the house, it did grow inky black, and the girls instinctively huddled together.

"I think here is good," announced Phoebe, stopping halfway up the hill. "Let's just light them here and then we can go back."

"No, we need to go to the top." Sloan was firm, and Neeve was torn. Sloan definitely had something in mind, and Neeve had to find out what it was.

"Come on, Bee. Let's just get it over with," instructed Neeve. She wasn't going to back down now and let Sloan Bicket call her a chicken for the rest of the summer. Nor was she going to stand for Sloan's possibly knowing more about The Sound than she did, although how Sloan would know that kind of thing, Neeve couldn't imagine. Had Sheila told her stuff? Unlikely. Sloan's dad? Hmm . . . Maybe. "Anyway, Bee, it's just Gee's property. It's not like there's some crazy guy with a hatchet living out here."

Phoebe squeaked in fear and turned on her heel. She fled

back to the Dorm, crashing through the bushes so they could hear her all the way back.

Neeve turned to the others. "Okay, it's just the three of us," she said brightly. But she did have that sinking feeling she'd get when watching a horror movie where the characters are about to go somewhere they shouldn't, and she'd want to yell at the screen, *"No! Don't go! Turn back!"* Fear made her even angrier at Sloan. "Where are we going, Sloan?" she demanded.

"Just to the top of the hill," said Sloan casually over her shoulder.

"But why?" pressed Neeve finally, wondering why she hadn't demanded to know earlier.

"There's something my dad told me about up here and I wanted to see for myself if it was true," said Sloan.

"What *is* it?" Neeve had lost all patience.

"You'll see," said Sloan in such an annoying way that Neeve wanted to kill her.

"This is dumb," said Neeve. "Let's go back."

"We're almost there!" protested Hillary, always one for adventure. "Come on, Neeve. Don't you want to see whatever it is?"

"Curiosity killed the cat," spat Neeve, but she sighed a big, annoyed sigh and kept on going. "All I can say is it better be worth it," she muttered.

The girls trudged up the hill, whacking aside blooming honeysuckle vines that draped in their way, and drawing close together in a tight little bunch. Neeve was almost tempted to ask Hillary if she could hold her hand, but she shuddered at the dorkiness of such an idea and made herself be brave. The lights from their flashlights bumped up and down, and Neeve did what she always did when she got scared: She sang "Tainted Love" in her head. It was an old eighties song that had been reborn into popularity at school dances in Shanghai, and something about its rhythm always made her feel better.

A moment or two later, they reached a clearing that seemed to be the top of the hill.

"Is this it?" asked Neeve, unimpressed. She couldn't make out much at first.

"I think so. Quick! Light the sparklers!" said Sloan.

Neeve dropped her flashlight and pulled the matches from her pocket. Hillary doled out three sparklers each and Neeve lit them all with one match.

"Ow!" she cried, shaking her hand where a tiny spark had hit her.

They looped the sparklers around in the air, and it did look really cool. Neeve traced her name in the dark and the illumination seemed to hang there, so she could see her name floating.

Then something caught her eye.

Her sparklers sizzled out and she bent to retrieve her flashlight, careful to keep hold of the still-warm-sparkler lest it drop and start a fire.

"Hey . . ." Neeve shone her flashlight across the wide arc of the clearing.

All around them, lined up in a circle, was a series of small, vaguely rectangular rocks.

"Stonehenge!" cried Neeve.

"I think it's a graveyard," whispered Hillary, and then they could all see that she was right.

"It is," whispered Sloan. Suddenly, she didn't seem as confident as she had before.

"What?! You knew about this?" Neeve was freaked out. Why would there be a graveyard on Gee's property? And why would Sloan know about it and not them?

"Creepy!" said Hillary.

"Why did you bring us up here?" asked Neeve.

"I wanted to see if it was true. Sometimes my dad teases me about stuff and I couldn't tell if he was serious this time. He was like, 'Watch out for that graveyard . . . the Callahans like to bury their dead right there on their own land . . .'"

"No way!" scoffed Neeve. "There couldn't be people buried here!"

Hillary aimed her flashlights around at the stones one by one.

"Are there any names on the stones?" asked Neeve nervously.

"Nope, nope, no, uh-huh, oh . . . here's one. 'Alfred Edward Callahan. 1968–1973. Our Beloved Baby,'" she read aloud. "Yikes!" she yelped.

"What?!" cried Neeve, backing away. "There are dead babies buried in here?" She flashed her light at the grave Hillary was reading and saw the words. And as she turned on her heel to flee, her light caught a name on one other: *Castell.*

Neeve shrieked and bolted, flailing blindly through the woods back in the direction from which they'd come.

Sloan and Hillary quickly followed suit, hooting and hollering.

Neeve had never been so freaked out in her life. She could feel herself shaking as she ran, and her teeth were chattering like maracas in her head. She was completely unaware of her surroundings as she ran; she just aimed toward the dim light in the distance and raced forward, with Sloan and Hillary hot on her heels.

▲

Neeve burst into the Dorm, wild-eyed and disheveled, with leaves and honeysuckle flowers stuck in her hair.

Phoebe and Kate were sitting side by side on the sofa, but Neeve didn't notice that they weren't actually doing anything. They were just sitting.

Neeve launched into a rambling account about graves and dead babies, and Hillary came bounding in the door a second later. The two of them were speaking at top volume, one over the other, and Phoebe and Kate couldn't make any sense of what they were saying. Finally, Phoebe yelled, "Silence!" at the top of her lungs and they both shut up and looked at her.

"Look, I don't care what you saw or what happened up there. We have something much more serious to discuss."

Neeve couldn't imagine what could be more serious than a hill full of dead people, especially including one that was, apparently, her father's former wife. But something about Phoebe's tone made her stay quiet.

"Where is Sloan?" demanded Phoebe.

Neeve and Hillary looked around the room, suddenly noticing that Sloan wasn't with them.

"I don't know. She was right behind us. Maybe she took the long route?" suggested Hillary.

"Actually, I really don't care where she is," snapped Neeve.

"Whatever," said Phoebe. "Look what we found while you were gone." She held up a white card with words printed on it.

Neeve squinted to see what it said, but she couldn't make it out. "What is it?" she said finally.

"It was in Sloan's bag," said Kate quietly.

Neeve's eyes widened. "Were you going through her stuff?"

"No," said Phoebe in a withering voice. "We were going up to the tower to see if we could see you guys up there on the hill, and Kate tripped over Sloan's wide-open suitcase and this popped out."

Neeve turned and looked at Kate; instantly she saw that Kate's eyes were wide with fear. Neeve's heart dropped even further, and she gulped.

"What is it?" Her nerves were frayed as it was. She couldn't take one more fright tonight.

Phoebe took a deep breath and crossed the room to Neeve. "Here," she said, holding out the card. "See for yourself."

Neeve took the card and looked down at it. It was thick, cream-colored, and rectangular, like a wedding invitation, only much smaller. Printed in dark blue ink was the prayer of Saint Francis of Assisi.

Neeve read it and looked up at Phoebe in confusion. "Yeah?"

Phoebe looked at her with sadness in her eyes. "Flip it over," she said quietly.

And Neeve did. Silently she read the words, and tears sprang to her eyes. "Oh!" she gasped. "It *is* true, after all!"

"What is it?" Hillary's voice was full of fear.

Neeve couldn't answer, so Kate took a deep breath.

"It's a funeral card. A memorial card," explained Kate softly. "For Serena Castell. Serena Castell *Callahan*. She's dead."

CHAPTER FOURTEEN

An Emergency

"What?!" yelled Hillary. She tripped across the room to where Neeve was standing, still clutching the card, and grabbed it to inspect it herself.

All the color had drained out of Neeve's face. Neeve could feel the blood throbbing in her temples, and she felt like she was going to be sick. Finally, she sank down and sat on the floor. Sloan had said everyone on Gull had been so upset; she must've meant when Serena died. And now only one thought kept going through Neeve's mind: *Did he kill her? Did he kill her? Did he kill her?* pounding in time with her heart.

Neeve looked up at the others and finally managed a strangled whisper. She needed to know what they thought. "Do you think he killed her?" she gulped.

She saw Hillary's jaw drop in shock, and Phoebe's eyes widen.

"No," Kate said firmly, and gave a vigorous shake of her

head. "No way. Anyway, he'd have still been in jail. We'd know." Kate watched tons of crime shows (even though they terrified her, she just couldn't turn away), so she knew a lot about murder and its punishment.

"How can you be so sure?" asked Neeve. "I mean, it all adds up . . ." Her imagination was reeling with possibilities. She put her head in her hands, holding it as if to keep it from exploding.

Hillary frowned. "What all adds up?"

"The sad ending, everyone on Gull upset, my dad living in foreign countries all the time, Mrs. Castell saying something was painful, Serena's turning out to be dead, the grave . . ."

"Wait just a second! What the heck are you *talking* about?!" shouted Hillary. "Have you lost your *mind*?!"

Neeve took a deep breath. "Okay, well, you know Sloan told me that the marriage ended badly and everyone was sad . . ."

"Yeah." The others nodded. "But what's all this about Mrs. Castell and a grave?" asked Hillary.

Neeve related the conversation she'd heard in the pharmacy earlier, and the girls were silent and breathless during the account.

"Whoa!" breathed Hillary. "Major!"

Neeve nodded.

"Poor you!" added Phoebe.

"And the grave? What's that part?" asked Kate, ever the morbid one.

Hillary and Neeve began to describe what they'd seen up on

the hill, all the graves, and the "Beloved Baby" one in particular. Then Neeve told them the name she saw on the stone as she was racing away. Castell.

"You don't think that's your father's first wife buried up there, do you? For real?" Kate was incredulous.

"I don't know . . ." Neeve was unsure. "But who else could it be?"

"It's weird that Sloan knew about the graveyard and we didn't," said Phoebe, tapping her chin pensively.

"Hey, where *is* Sloan?" said Hillary abruptly. "She should have been back here by now."

"You're right," agreed Neeve, suddenly worried. "She was with you, wasn't she?"

Hillary nodded. "Yeah, I know she made it out of the trees with me. But when it opened up, I got running so fast I wasn't paying attention."

"Where could she go at this hour?" Phoebe looked at her watch. It was past eleven.

"And how?" added Kate.

"I'll go look for her," volunteered Neeve wearily. "I feel like it's my fault we're in this whole mess, anyway."

Neeve stepped out of the Dorm, grabbing a flashlight on the way. "Sloan?" she whispered loudly into the dimness of the tiny lawn surrounding the Dorm. "Sloan?!"

Neeve exited through the gate in the hedge and retraced her footsteps toward the hill, but there was no sign of Sloan. She made her way across the side lawn, over to the patio, and into the kitchen, which was dark except for the light over the sink. No Sloan.

She wouldn't have gone upstairs, would she? thought Neeve. Sloan didn't know the house, and that would be a pretty bold move. Neeve whispered Sloan's name aloud, but there was no response. She decided to go out the front door and down the driveway. Maybe Sloan was walking home.

Neeve walked quietly, careful not to make any noise. She didn't want to wake up Gee and drag her into this whole thing. She crept through the house to the front hall, and creaked open the front door. Then she stepped out on the front step and pulled the door gently shut behind her.

"Sloan?" she whispered.

Suddenly something caught her eye. She looked closely.

It was Sloan. In Gee's car. In the driver's seat. Neeve gasped. *No!*

At the exact same moment, Sloan saw Neeve. In a panic, she turned the ignition, and the engine started. And before Neeve could call out, Gee's car began to roll slowly down the driveway.

Neeve gave a little yelp and ran across the driveway, lifting her bare feet high as she stepped, to minimize the agony of running on the broken seashells that paved the driveway.

Luckily, Sloan was a tentative driver, and Neeve an adroit pursuer. She caught up to the car quickly and banged on the window. Sloan managed to bring the car to a jerky stop. Neeve gestured for Sloan to roll the window down, and Sloan fumbled for a moment, and then the window squeaked open.

"Sloan! Are you crazy? What are you doing?!" Neeve was wild with fright. This was the most dangerous thing she'd ever seen anyone do.

"I'm going home," said Sloan calmly.

"You can't drive this car! You're only twelve!"

"Your grandmother lets you guys drive it," said Sloan rationally, and she began to roll the window back up.

Neeve yanked the driver's side door handle and the door swung open. Sloan panicked and gunned the accelerator, but her other foot was still on the brake, so the car didn't move.

Neeve paused for a moment, and then began to speak like she was trying to persuade a frightened animal out of a tree. "Okay, Sloan. Put the car into park. Nice and easy. Just move over and *I* will drive you home." Neeve worked hard to exude confidence and capability. She needed Sloan to trust her.

Sloan looked at her skeptically, then seemed to wilt. "Fine," she muttered, and she struggled with the gear shift momentarily while she maneuvered it into park. Finally, she slid over to the passenger seat.

Neeve got in. She hadn't thought this far ahead, so now she wasn't sure what to do. She buckled up her seatbelt as a matter of habit, then took the wheel with both hands. She took a deep breath, pushed the brake with her foot, and . . . The porch lights came on.

Neeve turned in time to see Gee, in her bathrobe, fling open the front door and march down the steps and across the driveway.

"Uh-oh," said Sloan, just as Gee flung open Neeve's door.

"Neeve Callahan, step out here this minute!" yelled Gee in a voice of strangled fury.

Neeve cringed. She'd never seen Gee so mad before. She unbuckled her seatbelt, turned off the engine, and climbed out of the driver's seat.

Gee ducked her head to look into the car. "And you too, Sloan!" she scolded.

Sloan sheepishly got out of the car and came around to stand by Neeve.

Gee was fuming. "I have never been so angry in all of my life!" she declared. "Come inside this instant!"

Sloan and Neeve began skulking guiltily toward the front door, with Gee following closely behind. The only sound was the emphatic crunching of Gee's slippers on the driveway, and the pounding of Neeve's heart in her ears.

"Now, march! Into the kitchen, and we'll get to the bottom of all this!" directed Gee.

A moment later, Sloan and Neeve sat at the banquette in the kitchen, and Gee was at the head of the table in her usual chair. The girls hung their heads in shame, and Gee just looked at them, her elbows propped on the table and her hands folded under her chin.

Finally, she sighed heavily. "Okay, who would like to tell me what you two were doing in the car?"

Sloan and Neeve glanced at each other. Neither one knew

CONTENTS

3 INDUSTRY AND COMPETITIVE ANALYSIS 68

4 EVALUATING COMPANY RESOURCES AND COMPETITIVE CAPABILITIES 103

5 STRATEGY AND COMPETITIVE ADVANTAGE 134

*Cases for which there are case preparation exercises on Strat-TUTOR.

where to begin, nor how much to confess. Finally, Neeve took a deep breath.

"It's my fault, Gee. I was driving Sloan home."

Gee was incredulous. "You know very well that you're not to drive anytime, anywhere, unless it's an absolute emergency."

"Well, it sort of was . . ." Neeve trailed off. She wasn't a great liar.

Gee looked at her sternly. "Of what sort?"

"Actually, Mrs. Callahan, it was all my fault." Sloan had finally found her voice. Neeve looked at Sloan in surprise; she'd been sure Sloan would let her take the rap for this.

"Go on," said Gee.

"Well, I got really scared, and I, like, ran away, and I was trying to drive myself home . . . and Neeve kind of rescued me."

"Mmm-hmmm . . . ," Gee encouraged.

Neeve looked at Gee. "It's true. I made her move over so I could get in the driver's seat. I wasn't sure what I'd do next, but then you came out, so I didn't have to decide."

"I'm quite sure you would have made the decision to park the car and come get me," said Gee. "Right?"

"Yeah." Neeve nodded. Now that Gee said it like that, it was obvious that she would have done that. She could picture herself doing it, pocketing the car keys and marching up the stairs. She nodded once again for emphasis.

"And what was the nature of the emergency?" prodded Gee.

"Oh. Uh . . ." Neeve didn't know where to begin.

"I got scared by the graveyard," Sloan said flatly. "And I wanted to go home."

Gee looked confused. "What graveyard? Where?"

Neeve got the chills all over again, just thinking of the three of them up there in the dark, surrounded by dead people. And just then, the door to the patio opened and Neeve jumped, but it was only Kate, Phoebe, and Hillary.

"What's up?" asked Hillary. The three girls slid onto the long banquette and looked questioningly from Gee to Sloan and Neeve, then back again.

"I'm not sure myself," said Gee. "All I know so far is that I found these two in the car, preparing for a drive, and now I'm hearing about an emergency in a graveyard."

There was a long silence, while everyone digested this information. The four cousins looked at one another, and finally, Neeve took a deep breath.

"Gee?" she began. "Why don't you tell us about Serena Castell."

CHAPTER FIFTEEN
Good Riddance

Gee gasped. "Oh, my," she said, and she put her hand to her chest.

Kate looked at her in concern. "Are you alright?" she asked.

Gee smiled weakly. "Yes. You just gave me a surprise, that's all. I haven't heard that name around this house for years." Then her eyes misted up, and she shook her head impatiently and reached for a handkerchief in her pocket. The girls exchanged glances and waited quietly while she dabbed at her eyes. *I guess Callahans do cry*, thought Neeve distractedly. *So there!*

Finally, Gee took a big breath and released it. This seemed to compose her.

"I'll tell you what. Why don't I go upstairs and throw on something decent so I can take Sloan home. Meanwhile, go gather Sloan's things, and Sloan, you meet me at the car, okay? Girls, we'll talk just as soon as I get back."

"Okay . . . ," the girls agreed. Gee never cried, nor did she ever send guests home. It must be something serious to warrant both of these reactions.

Gee rose to go upstairs, but then she turned back, wagging her finger at the group. "You're not off the hook for trying to drive my car, yet. We'll get to that later." Neeve gulped as she stood to walk back to the Dorm.

The girls filed silently out of the kitchen, but once they were about halfway down the yard, they began whispering madly.

"What do you think?"

"This is majorly major!"

"I can't even imagine."

But Neeve didn't speak. She felt numb, hanging in limbo, awaiting the full story — assuming that was what Gee would give them.

When they reached the Dorm, Phoebe's anger at Sloan reignited. "Why did you bring that memorial card here?" she demanded.

Standing at the foot of the ladder to the loft, Sloan was stunned. "Did you go through my stuff?"

"Like we'd bother," sniffed Phoebe. She perched on the arm of the couch and explained how they'd happened upon the card. "Were you just trying to think of ways to upset Neeve at her own party? Is that why you brought it here?"

"I brought that card because it seemed like Neeve didn't know that Serena was dead. So when I found the card in our junk basket, I guessed she'd want to see it."

"Were you trying to be nice or to just upset her?" grilled Phoebe.

"To be nice!" protested Sloan. "I swear!"

"So how did Serena die?" pressed Hillary.

"I have no idea. I never asked," stated Sloan somberly.

"I don't believe that for one second," spat Phoebe.

"It's true!" Sloan looked worried. "I can't talk to my mom about it because . . . well . . . she's mad at me, about the trade. She found out that I took Neeve's makeup for the photos and she called me a . . . profiteer."

"What's that?" said Kate.

"I don't even know!" wailed Sloan.

"Someone who makes a living off other people's misery," answered Phoebe with a withering glance at Sloan. "An apt description, I might add."

At the far end of the couch, Neeve had sunk into the cushions in exhaustion. She knew she should reveal the real contents of the white shopping bag at this moment, but she couldn't bring herself to do so. Instead, she watched as Sloan winced at Phoebe's comment, and she kept her mouth shut.

Phoebe turned back to Neeve. "Look, it's only a little while longer, and then we'll know the whole story. Just be patient, okay?"

Neeve was too shell-shocked to be anything but patient. She curled up into a ball and stared blankly at the assembled group.

"I'll just get my stuff," said Sloan.

"You do that," said Phoebe. Phoebe had been growing into the role of Neeve's defender for some time now, and Neeve smiled weakly at how well the formerly reluctant socializer was handling it.

After Sloan had climbed the ladder, Kate whispered, "Bee, be nice. You're being too hard on Sloan."

"Baloney!" said Phoebe in full voice, so they all knew Sloan could hear. "It's her fault that this is all happening. She's the one who dragged everyone up to the graveyard. She's the one who tried to drive Gee's car, am I right?" She looked at Neeve.

Neeve spoke wearily. "I should have never let this Serena thing go so far. I should've just asked Gee about it when I found that first photo."

"Yeah," said Hillary. "Family secrets are dangerous. You don't want to play with fire."

Neeve sat up, energized momentarily by what she felt was an unjust accusation. "I didn't *play* with anything!" she said, slapping her hand on the couch cushion for emphasis.

"No, but you know what I mean . . . ," said Hillary.

Sloan came down the ladder, her tightly zipped bag over her shoulder.

Phoebe looked at her with disdain. "Anything else in there you'd like us to see?' she asked.

"No," Sloan said quietly.

Neeve looked at Sloan, then decided to take the bull by the

horns. "Sloan, why are you sometimes so nice to us and sometimes so nasty? We don't get it."

The others were shocked, even Phoebe, that Neeve had been so blunt. But they all looked at Sloan to see what she'd say.

She thought for a moment. Then, "I don't know," she said honestly, shrugging. "I'm not sure myself. Sometimes I like you guys and I want to be your friend, but other times you're so cliquey and superior and exclusive that you make me sick." Her eyes flashed with anger.

"Down, girl!" laughed Neeve, for the first time in what felt like days. The others weren't sure what to say. Sloan didn't crack a smile.

"I guess we feel the same way about you," said Kate quietly.

"Although you're much meaner to us than we ever were to you," added Phoebe.

Now it was Sloan's turn to shrug. "Whatever. Sorry." She crossed the room to the door, and put her hand on the handle.

"Which is it, 'whatever' or 'sorry'?" pressed Phoebe.

"I'm not sure," said Sloan, and she opened the door and left.

"Good riddance," muttered Phoebe, as the door closed behind Sloan.

The girls were quiet after Sloan left. No one knew what to say. Neeve curled back up into a ball, her last drop of energy spent on the confrontation with Sloan.

"So was Sloan really trying to drive Gee's car?" asked Hillary after a while.

Neeve nodded mutely.

"Wow." Hillary was half-horrified and half-impressed. She was silent while she tried to picture the scene.

"Was Gee furious?" asked Kate.

"Uh-huh," murmured Neeve.

They all digested this bit of information, each imagining being on the receiving end of Gee's anger. It was difficult to process.

After a little bit, Phoebe said, "Should we go back up and wait for Gee?"

No one said anything. Phoebe glanced at Neeve, but she'd fallen asleep on the couch. She looked at Kate, then Hillary.

"Maybe one of us should go leave a note for Gee, saying we can talk in the morning."

Hillary stood up. "I will. Are we sleeping here?"

Kate nodded, and Phoebe stood up and began turning off lights. Kate went up to the loft to grab a blanket for Neeve, then came back down to cover her up. She lifted Neeve's legs gently out from under her, and repositioned her so she was stretched out on the couch. Neeve mumbled something and rolled over, but she didn't wake up.

"She's wiped out," whispered Kate to Phoebe.

"Yeah."

"Goodnight, Neeve," whispered Kate. But there was no reply.

CHAPTER SIXTEEN

Donuts and Revelations

Saturday morning, Neeve awoke at dawn. She wasn't sure where she was at first, or why, but then it all came flooding back to her. She must've fallen asleep on the couch, and the others had let her stay there.

"Oh my God," she whispered, as the events of the night before came flooding back to her. Gee was going to kill her. But first she was going to tell her about Serena.

There was no way Neeve could go back to sleep now. She swung her legs over the edge of the couch and blinked a few times. Coffee. She needed coffee.

She stretched and rose, then quietly let herself out of the Dorm and climbed the cold, dew-covered lawn to the kitchen. Sheila and Gee weren't even up yet, which was a rarity. Neeve glanced at the clock. Five-thirty! She looked back out at the sky. She'd thought it was later. She fiddled with the coffeemaker, then sat at the kitchen table, perfectly still, while the machine slurped noisily, going about its job.

She was well into her second cup by the time Sheila came down. Sheila was surprised to see her. She frowned at the coffee pot (Sheila thought Neeve was too young for coffee; she didn't realize that in a lot of the places Neeve had been, it was the only safe thing — sometimes the only thing — to drink. Neeve had had to acquire a taste for it at an early age). Luckily for Neeve, Sheila wasn't a big talker first thing in the morning, so she wasn't stuck explaining anything about why she was there, nor did she have to make silly small talk about the weather or anything. Sheila just went about her morning routine, emptying the dishwasher, rolling out the dough for sticky buns, and so on.

At six-thirty, Gee appeared in her terry cloth toweling robe. Neeve was partially relieved and partially terrified to see her. She wasn't sure how mad Gee still was, nor was she sure she wanted to hear the story of Serena Castell. But now there was no way she could just put it all behind her and move on. She was too entangled.

Gee was only momentarily surprised to see Neeve up so early. She poured herself a cup of coffee, added milk, then came to sit by Neeve at the table. She smiled, and Neeve relaxed. Maybe it wouldn't be so bad.

Gee took a sip of her coffee and said, "Why don't we go for a drive?"

Neeve nodded.

"Let me just go take off my bathing suit and put on some clothes, alright?" And Neeve nodded again. Things were really serious if Gee was giving up her morning swim.

Gee was back in a flash, and she called goodbye to Sheila in the laundry room. Then she and Neeve walked out to her car and climbed in.

"Donuts first?" suggested Gee, and Neeve nodded. They drove in silence, except for the radio, all the way into town, and Gee pulled up in front of the News Co., which sold locally famous hot cinnamon donuts that they made in an old-fashioned donut machine in their window.

"Be right back," said Gee, and she ducked inside.

Gee returned with a paper bag full of donuts, a couple of orange juices, and two more coffees. She handed it all to Neeve, and Neeve put the bag on her lap, shifting it often to move the hot patches around. Then Gee drove them out to Macaroni Beach, pulled into a parking spot at the top so they could watch the ocean, and turned off the car. Serena's name hung unspoken in the air, like a heavy fog. Neeve had no idea what to expect. She steeled herself against the bad news and vowed to try and love her father, still, no matter what she discovered.

Mechanically, Neeve doled out the food, and they ate a bit, and then Gee said, "Let's put aside the events of last night for a little while, shall we?"

Neeve nodded nervously.

Then Gee sighed and said, "Alright. Serena, then. I'm not sure where to begin, so I'm going to just tell you the story from the beginning."

Neeve nodded again, her stomach bunched with anxiety. She wanted to hear, but she also didn't want to hear what Gee had to tell her.

"Mind you," said Gee, "Your father should really be telling you this story, because it's his to tell. You'll need to call him later today to have him give you his perspective."

"Okay." Neeve nodded solemnly and gulped. This didn't sound good. Her skin began to prickle with dread, and Gee began the story.

"Serena Castell was one of the most beautiful, bewitching, fun, lively creatures I have ever met in my life." Gee folded her arms and looked at Neeve. "You know the sort of person who creates fun wherever they go? And you just want to be around them all the time so that you don't miss a moment of it?" Neeve nodded. "That was her.

"The Castells began coming here in the summertime when your father was about fifteen. They'd rent the Murray place, just over a street from us, and they had a big brood, too. We knew them a bit from the city, because Sandy and John were very active in a lot of organizations that Pops and I were involved in, but they lived in Newton, so we didn't see them much. Anyhow, of all the children in both families, your father and Serena were enchanted by one another. Right from the start." Gee smiled at the memory. "I've always said that one look at them confirmed for me the notion of love at first sight. They couldn't get enough of each other. Serena just delighted Bill, and he followed her around like a puppy dog, even though she was a year or two younger than him. And she thought he was a god; she just worshipped him. Your father was always very dashing and charismatic, you know, ever since he was a baby."

Neeve smiled. It was still true. People loved him. Even some of her friends had crushes on him.

"And he was so kind to her, so careful to take care of her," Gee was thoughtful. "Just like he is with everyone . . ."

Neeve's smile faded. Was he always kind to Serena? She didn't know where this story was heading.

Gee went on. "So they dated very seriously that first summer, and when the summer ended — oh! — it was like a Shakespearean tragedy. Star-crossed lovers, each returning to boarding schools in different states, 'When will we see each other again?' and all that. I can laugh a little bit about it now, but at the time, it was such high drama. You'd think they were parting for life rather than just a few months, because after all their homes in Newton and Boston were only minutes apart; they could organize to see each other when they came home for long weekends, or vacations. But the boarding school distance made them drift apart each winter. They'd date other people, then see each other on vacation and get back together; it was always some drama, breaking up, reuniting! But then in the summers, those embers were fanned, and it was full-blown inferno of love again." Gee giggled. "Oh my word, teenage love! They should bottle it! In any case, this pattern persisted for them all through boarding school, and then on into college." Gee glanced at Neeve. "I know this story seems long, but you need to know the full history of it all."

"No, go on, I'm . . . entranced." That was the only word Neeve could think of. And she was. It was a happy story, so far.

"Okay, so Bill and Serena. They were simply wonderful together, always doing interesting things, having parties, making unique friends, traveling to ungodly places as they got older — you know your father and his obsession with the ends of the earth!"

Neeve laughed and nodded. "Yeah."

"Well, you know, as a mother, you figure, ah, first love. It will probably end one day, and they'll end up married to other people, running into each other in some strange place like an airport, laughing about old times, and that's it. But no! These two just lasted and lasted. And really, I can tell you now, I was so pleased. Sandy Castell and I confessed to each other that we always wanted them to stay together — or get back together during those times they were apart — because they were so good for each other. But you know, a mother mustn't ever get involved in her children's romantic life. It's just a bad idea. Plus I figured if I told Bill how much we all adored Serena, he'd do something silly like run the other way. So I kept my mouth shut and my fingers crossed."

Gee was quiet, remembering the happy years of Neeve's dad's courtship of Serena.

"And?" Neeve prodded after a moment. She knew things had to go wrong, sooner or later. She felt sick with wanting to know.

"Oh, well. Then the most wonderful thing happened. Bill came to me and said he wanted to marry Serena, and would I help him pick out a ring? I was beside myself! I thought it was right out of a fairy tale! So we went home to Boston, to my jeweler, and Bill designed the most exquisite ring. And when it was ready, he picked it up and brought it back to Gull. It was just the Friday of Labor Day weekend, and he meant to propose to Serena at our Labor Day party, after he'd asked her father, of course. But when he got back to Gull, Serena wasn't there. Her parents and she had gone into Boston — they'd practically crossed Bill on the ferry as they went over — and her brothers and sisters, whom Bill kept interrogating, poor things — weren't sure why. It was something vague about a checkup, or a dentist appointment. They each had a different story, and frankly, they didn't know themselves; but they were sure she'd be back Sunday. Well! Your poor father! He was devastated. Serena had left without telling him anything, and all of his plans for the engagement weekend were dashed. He kept trying to call her in Newton, only no one answered — this was before everyone had answering machines, you know. So he was frantic. Finally, that Saturday morning, I told him to go there. To go and find her." Gee paused and put her hand over her eyes, as if the memory was too much to bear.

"Gee?" whispered Neeve. "Are you okay?"

Gee took a long ragged breath. "Yes." She cleared her throat.

"So what happened? I mean, did he go? Did he find her?" Neeve prompted.

"Yes. He did. It turned out that she had been feeling poorly for some time, but she'd put it down to graduating from college, and all the excitement and stress that came with it. But you know, she was so amazing — she just sort of hid it from the rest of us. Well, finally, her parents had had enough. They dragged her into Boston to see some specialist, and they discovered that she had advanced leukemia."

Neeve gasped. "That's cancer, right?"

"Right. Cancer of the blood. And they'd begun treatment immediately, that very day. The doctor was desperate to do anything to try to save her, but his prognosis was grim. And no one had had a chance to call Bill and tell him, because Serena was just out of it and her parents didn't know what to say, or how. Bill arrived at their house in Newton and was directed to the hospital by a sister of Sandy's who'd come to stay when she'd heard the news. Well, you can imagine your father as he raced to the hospital to find her. Her aunt hadn't told him what it was, she'd just told him where they were."

Gee put her face in her hands. "The poor child. He was wild! Wild with grief!"

Neeve's eyes welled up with tears, thinking of her father as a young man, receiving this devastating news. "So what happened?"

Gee sighed. "Well, there was a great deal of treatment, and the engagement fell by the wayside for a while, while they focused on anything that might make her well again. Then Bill asked her to marry him, and Serena thought he was only asking her out of pity, and she kept refusing him. She didn't believe that Bill had wanted to marry her before the diagnosis, didn't believe he wanted to marry her still, in spite of the diagnosis. He was just beside himself; didn't know what to do. After a bit, though, she seemed to improve a little, physically, and her outlook improved with it, and he finally convinced her to marry him. So, the next summer, we held a wonderful wedding here on Gull, at our house, actually, and the two were married." Gee smiled at the memory, and then her face darkened. "Nine months later, Serena . . . died."

"Oh my God!" cried Neeve. "That is so sad!" Huge tears welled out of her eyes, and she couldn't begin to check them. Gee cried too and doled out hankies and then paper napkins, as the hankies grew sodden.

"It was just awful. We never thought he'd recover. We thought none of us would ever recover!" Gee shook her head and sighed a shuddery sigh. "But, you know, he threw himself into his work, and he's done so magnificently well. And then he finally met your mother — the only woman he'd dated since Serena — and we all held our breath until they actually walked down the aisle. Your mother brought him back to life, and I bless her for it every day. And then you! His wonderful children! He absolutely lives for you!"

But Neeve was confused. "So why didn't he ever mention Serena to us before?"

Gee looked at her gently. "You know, it is still so painful for him. And I can imagine that it really never has come up, conversationally, with you three. It's a pretty heavy piece of news to deliver to a child, especially when you don't want to upset them. I'm sure he meant to tell you in his own time." Gee reached for Neeve's hand and held it comfortingly.

They sat in silence for a minute, watching the waves.

And then Neeve said tentatively, "And she's buried at your house?"

Gee burst out laughing, her eyes wide with shock. "What?! *No!* Of course not! She's buried in the Catholic graveyard in town! What ever gave you that idea?"

Neeve was confused. "But last night, Sloan took us up the hill . . . and there was the graveyard . . . and I saw 'Castell' . . . and then we ran . . . and I just . . ." She was tripping over her words, trying to explain. Meanwhile, Gee had stopped laughing. She was shaking her head.

"No, no, *no!* I know what you found! It's that ridiculous pet cemetery! I was wondering what all that graveyard talk was about last night!"

"Pet cemetery? Then who is Alfred Edward Callahan? 'Our beloved Baby'?"

Gee's hand flew to cover her mouth. "Oh, my dear! No wonder you were spooked! Baby was one of Kathy's dogs that we had to put down one summer. His official name from the breeder was Alfred Edward Callahan, but we all called him Baby." Gee laughed again, incredulous. "Did you think it was one of my *children*?"

"Well, I didn't know . . . ," said Neeve, not amused at all. "I mean, it *looked* like a regular grave, a people grave."

"Oh, my, I am sorry! But what gave you the idea that Serena was buried there?"

"One of the graves said 'Castell.'"

Gee was quiet for a moment; then she remembered. "No, that was one of Serena's brother's hamsters or something! Oh, for Lord's sake. I knew that pet cemetery was a terrible idea. But your father and uncles got it in their heads to go ahead with it, and, well, it did keep them occupied and out of my hair from time to time."

Neeve smiled shakily. "Oh."

"But you said Sloan had taken you up there? Why?"

"Her father had told her that there was a graveyard at your house — that 'the Callahans bury their dead on their own property' or something. And she wanted to see if it was true. Then she got freaked out and ran away and tried to drive her-self home."

"Goodness. That explains what you were doing in the car, then."

"Yes." Neeve nodded and snuck a sidelong glance at Gee. It

didn't seem like Gee was mad at her about the car anymore. "Am I still in trouble?" Neeve ventured.

"No. Sloan actually convinced me that it was all her fault as I drove her home. She never quite spelled out what had gotten you to that point, but I did end up convinced you had nothing to do with it. Needless to say, when a Callahan and a Bicket are at odds, I'm always likely to take the Callahan side." Gee smiled and tousled Neeve's hair. "But you must swear to me that you will never, ever drive a car until you are the legal age."

"But what about emergencies?" Neeve was indignant. She was so pleased at her driving abilities that she was eager to put them to use for a good cause. In fact, she was hoping for an emergency so she could show off.

"Well, if a grown-up tells you that it's an emergency and orders you to drive a car, then that's fine. It's just that sometimes young people have a hard time deciding what's an emergency and what's not." She winked at Neeve.

"Okay."

They paused and then Gee asked, "How did you find out about Serena anyhow?"

And Neeve related the whole story, from the photo in the attic, all the way up to overhearing Mrs. Castell at the drugstore the day before. Which now seemed like a million years ago.

"Oh, I didn't know they were here!" said Gee. "We haven't kept in such close touch for a few years, because after Serena died, they moved out West. I'm so happy to hear they're here. I must give Sandy a call. Did she look well?"

"Yes, she was really pretty," said Neeve.

"Like mother, like daughter," said Gee with a smile.

"They didn't have children, then?" asked Neeve suddenly, thinking of Mrs. Castell's grandchildren, waiting in the car.

"Who? Serena and Bill? No, no of course not. She wasn't well enough." Gee looked sharply at Neeve then. "You don't think your father would have had children and not raised them himself, did you?"

Of course Neeve had thought that, but she said, "No, no. Just checking."

Gee patted her hands on her knees once, then twice. "Well," she said. "Do you think we should get back to the others?"

"Yes. They're probably worried that you've strung me up somewhere as a punishment for last night." Neeve's eyes twinkled with mischief.

"Maybe we should make up a story . . ." Gee's eyes twinkled back, and she started the engine.

And as they drove back to The Sound, Neeve's heart lifted in a kind of giddy relief that flooded her with happiness. As she digested all of the new information, she smiled to herself. It was good to have her father back. Now she could love him again.

CHAPTER SEVENTEEN

A Hero

Neeve and Gee had hardly stepped out of the car when the cousins flew out of the front door and came to meet them. They all had questioning looks on their faces; they weren't sure what had happened — if Neeve was in trouble, if she was going to be sent home.

Neeve smiled at their concern and said, "It's alright. I'll explain everything."

"You're not in trouble then?" asked Kate.

"No. Sloan took the rap."

"As well she should have," said Phoebe.

"Wow! That's a surprise!" said Hillary.

Gee came around the car. "I'm so sorry we left you without a word. Neeve can tell you the story about our sweet Serena, and if you have any more questions, just ask. I'm happy to tell you about her."

The girls exchanged surprised looks, but they were clearly happy for Neeve.

"Now who would like to go to the beach with me for the morning?" suggested Gee brightly.

"Actually, we've still got some work to do, right guys?" said Neeve.

"Oh, of course, the reveal!" Gee laughed. "Okay, then I'll take a rain check. I'll be absolutely dying of suspense until tomorrow."

Alone, the girls tore down to the Dorm and settled themselves comfortably on the chairs and couches. There was no question of starting work until Neeve had related the whole Serena story to them. No one breathed a word as she told them the saga. And at the end, Kate had to go get Kleenex, she was crying so hard.

Neeve sat back against the couch cushions, wiped out by the retelling.

"I can't believe you thought your dad was a bad guy." Phoebe was shaking her head. "You only have to meet him once to know he wouldn't hurt a fly, let alone his own wife!"

Hillary was incredulous. "How about you thinking he killed her!" She shook her head.

"Well, I do have an active imagination. . . ." Neeve was ashamed of herself, and could hardly defend the thoughts she'd been thinking about her dad these past few weeks.

"Yeah, and not only was he not a bad guy, he was a *hero!*" wailed Kate, and the drama of her own statement sent her into a fresh shower of tears. The others shook their heads and laughed at her.

"You know, I really should call him." Neeve looked at her watch and did the automatic calculation to Irish time, as her dad would now be with her mum's family in Ireland. Would it be fair for her to call him there about Serena? Her mum's family must know about her already, and she really couldn't wait. But it was late afternoon there, and she knew her dad would be out on the golf course, just as surely as she knew anything. She decided to wait a couple of hours and call him then.

Instead, the girls threw themselves into finishing up the Dorm with renewed vigor. Neeve, in a huge burst of energy, was rearranging furniture, hanging pictures, finishing up projects, and generally running around like a chicken with her head cut off.

Hillary laughed at her at one point, and shook her head. "You do have style, girl. I can say that for you!"

Neeve laughed back. "It's more than I can say for you," she said in mock sympathy.

At noon, Neeve glanced at her watch. "I think I'm going to go call my dad now," she announced.

"Do you want us to come with you?" asked Kate in concern.

"Nah, I'll be fine. I think I should do it alone."

"Okay, then. Good luck!" and they sent her up the hill.

With trembling fingers, Neeve dialed her other grandmother's number at her summer house in Roundstone. Her grandmother answered, and they had a great "crack" (which is what the Irish call a chat), and then she went off in search of Neeve's dad.

But as soon as he got on the line, Neeve began to bawl. "Oh, Dad! I'm so sorry!"

Her father was a little frantic at first, not sure if Neeve was okay, but finally she convinced him that everything was fine, and she calmed herself down. She took a big, ragged breath and said, "I'm so sorry about Serena."

There was a dead silence down the line, and then, from miles away, in a barely audible voice, her dad said, "So you know, then?"

"Yes," said Neeve simply. "And I am so sorry, for you, for her, for everyone." And for everything bad that I thought about you, she added silently.

"Thanks, love," he said. "I am so sorry, too. And I'm sorry you found out before I had a chance to tell you myself."

"Kate thinks you're a hero!" added Neeve.

Her dad chuckled. "No, not a hero. Just a guy who was trying to take care of someone he loved, for his own selfish reasons, too."

And now that the ice was broken, Neeve was full of questions. She could hear her dad scraping one of her grandmother's kitchen chairs across the floor to her inconveniently placed telephone (the house was ancient and modern conveniences a necessary evil and an afterthought), and settling in for a good long talk. Neeve asked about their relationship,

Serena's family, whether he was sad he never had kids with her, whether he kept in touch with her parents. And he answered every question honestly and thoughtfully.

"You know, your aunt Jean was furious at me for marrying Serena," her dad admitted at one point. "We didn't speak for years because of it."

"You're kidding! Why?" Neeve's aunt Jean was her favorite of all her father's sisters. Fun, young (even though she had seven kids), a former nun, even. Neeve couldn't imagine her fighting with anyone.

"She thought I was trying to be a martyr, or a hero, to use Kate's word, or something. She thought I was ruining my life to prove a point, and that I was putting too much pressure on Serena, when she should have been only focusing on getting well. I guess I was being selfish, but I thought I could help her. I thought I could save her . . ." Her dad was choking back tears, and Neeve was horrified.

"Uh, Callahans don't cry, Dad!" she blurted, before she could stop herself.

Her father cleared his voice. "Rubbish! I know that's my own ridiculous ignorance coming back to bite me, and I'm sorry I ever started in with that nonsense. Of course Callahans cry; everyone cries, especially at very sad things. You know, when your mother and I began traveling with you kids, we were ignorant. Ignorant as parents and as expatriates, living all around the world. I just seized on that stupid phrase one day as a way of getting you kids to stop whining, and unfortunately it became a kind of family motto. Let's dump it now, though. Shall we? It really is utter blarney."

Neeve smiled at his use of the Irish word for silliness. "Okay," she agreed, smiling. "It hasn't really been working for me lately, anyway."

They chatted on, and then her father said, "I do go put flowers on Serena's grave every time I'm on Gull," he confessed. Neeve said she'd like to do that, too, and he said that was a lovely idea and he'd tell Gee to take her. "You know, you can see the Castells' house — the Murray house that the Castells rented — from the lookout tower in the Dorm. I used to go up there when I was feeling romantic or lovelorn, and if Serena stood on the widow's walk over there, we could wave to each other."

Neeve smiled at the image. She'd have to go up and look for herself.

"But did you love her more than mum?" she asked in a moment of bravery. She dreaded the answer.

"No, of course not. It was just different. We were so young," he said. "Children, practically. My God! And of course, your mother and I have been through so much together, lived so many places, had you wonderful kids. It's just very different. Your mother is . . . home to me."

Neeve thought about this for a minute. "Yeah, I know what you mean. When you're with the people you love most . . . when you can really be yourself, you're home."

"Yes," he said simply.

And then Neeve began filling him in on the Dorm, and her fights with Kate, and all the drama with Sloan.

"Goodness, what a lot you've been up to over there! It sounds like you're creating a wonderful home for yourself at Gee's."

"I am," admitted Neeve happily.

They chatted a bit longer and then began saying their good-byes. "I love you so much, Dad!" Neeve practically shouted. "I'm sending you a huge hug all the way across the ocean! *Tzai jen!*" Her Chinese vocabulary was getting rusty on Gull, but "goodbye" was easy enough to pull out.

"Thanks, pumpkin. And I'm glad you called. Thank Gee for me for explaining everything to you. Big hugs to you, and *wo ai ni!*" (Neeve laughed. *I love you* had been her first phrase in Chinese; it was not exactly useful on an everyday basis!) "Good luck with the Dorm!"

"Bye!"

Neeve felt like she'd burst with happiness as she hung up. She did have the best dad in the world, and he *was* a hero, just like Kate said. Imagine marrying someone who you knew was going to die soon. Even though it was a horrible, sad story, it made her love her dad more than ever.

And now, with no more distractions to keep her from her work on the Dorm, Neeve walked back down the hill, charged with the energy to finish creating her new home.

CHAPTER EIGHTEEN

The Reveal, for Real

Sunday morning at nine-thirty, the girls led Gee down the back lawn from the kitchen. The Dorm was ready and it was time for the reveal. They paused outside the door, told Gee to close her eyes, and then Kate flung open the door and shouted "Ta da!"

Gee gasped. "Oh my! Oh my!" was all she could say, at first. And then, "How wonderful! How clever!"

Inside, the Dorm was sparkling clean, with pillows fluffed, low bowls of fresh pink roses on the coffee table, and the wonderful smell of freesia room spray lingering in the air.

Gee stood just inside the doorway and turned this way and that, admiring every little detail: the trompe l'oeil area rug; the apple green coffee table; the two needlepoint throw cushions in pink and apple green; the blackboard wall (on which was scrawled HOME, SWEET HOME! in pink chalk); the fresh white slipcovers; the neat rows of family photographs in pink and green frames all along one wall; the new curtains and pink painted rods, the shiny white paint. Behind one of the couches was a tall table the girls had made from an ancient surfboard they'd found in the garage. They'd nailed wooden legs onto it and placed two lamps they'd found in the attic at either end, then added Hillary's iPod in the middle with little speakers. Gee couldn't believe they'd made the table themselves — she kept rubbing her hand along it and exclaiming how ingenious it was. She crossed the room to inspect the row of Chinese lanterns that hung from the loft, and then climbed the ladder to admire the sleeping area.

"What wonderful ideas you've all had," she admired.

"It was mostly Neeve," said Kate generously.

"Nah, it was mostly Kate," Neeve corrected.

"Phoebe and I were just the laborers," said Hillary with a smile.

Upstairs, the beds were neatly made with white sheets, and Kate had sewn little decorative pillows in pink-and-green-flowered Hawaiian-print fabric for each one. The banister across the edge of the loft was encrusted with pink glitter, which even Kate had had to admit looked really cool, and the bathroom mirror had a mosaic of fake pink jewels all around its frame. Each girl's dresser had a small basket for her things on top, and a family photograph in a pink Hawaiian-print frame. A green pegboard hung at one end on a wall, and the girls had neatly lined up straw sun hats on the pegs. Thin, bamboo beach mats lay on the floor between the beds as area rugs (Neeve had insisted they buy them at one of the junky tourist stores in town. They were so cheap and cool that she knew she had to have them, even before she knew what they'd use them for), and the lampshades were covered in hula-skirt grass (Neeve had won that battle after all).

The overall effect was of a really cool surfer girl hangout, and Gee was bowled over. At the end of the tour, Gee called for a celebration and announced they'd go to a special dinner that night at the Coolidge House hotel, which had the fanciest restaurant in town. The girls were thrilled at the idea, and Neeve began planning her outfit immediately. They all escorted Gee back down to the living room, and as the others answered more questions, Neeve's eye was caught by a photo in the rows of family pictures. It was the wedding picture she'd found that very first day of the Dorm project, the one of her dad and Serena. Someone had located it and hung it with the others. She still felt a jolt when she saw it.

Further down, following the chronological order in which Gee hung her own family photos in the big house, was a wedding picture of Neeve's dad and mum, at their wedding in Ireland. Neeve looked questioningly at the others, but Hillary and Phoebe were engrossed in a discussion of paint techniques with Gee. Then she looked at Kate, and Kate was smiling tentatively at her.

Neeve waved her across the room and Kate came. "Is it okay?" Kate whispered.

Neeve nodded. She had a little lump in her throat. "I

thought I was supposed to be the stylist!" She'd have to make a joke of it because she'd vowed last night as she went to sleep that she wouldn't cry again this summer, regardless of her dad's new take on crying; she'd already cried more in the last three weeks than she usually cried in a year or more, and it was enough.

Kate grinned. "I hope I did the right thing. I went and asked Sheila if she'd seen that photo, and she had. She was wondering how it had gotten there and she'd just put it away in the attic again in some random spot. I didn't say anything; I just asked her where it was. So I went and got it and dusted it off and brought it down here, and then I went looking for a picture of your parents that I could hang, too."

"Thanks. It was a really nice idea."

"I'm glad you like it." Kate beamed at Neeve and Neeve smiled back.

The girls officially moved in later that afternoon. It took a while to lug everything down, and they were crossing paths as they went in and out of the Dorm.

Neeve was upstairs putting her clothes away in her new dresser; she was an expert packer and unpacker so she usually flew through such tasks. But today, she was taking a little more time than usual so that everything would be just so. A knock on the door caught her attention.

"Come in!" called Neeve from upstairs, expecting Gee. She cocked her head to hear what Gee would say. But then she heard Phoebe's and Hillary's surprised "Hellos" and leaned over the railing to see who it was.

Sloan. Ugh. Neeve groaned inwardly. What could she want? Neeve hadn't laid eyes on her since that horrible night earlier in the weekend. She hoped Sloan wasn't here to see her.

But then, "Neeve?" Sloan was calling her in her nice voice. Neeve felt immediately suspicious.

"Up here," she replied cautiously.

"Can I come up?"

"Yup." What could Sloan possibly want?

A moment later, Sloan's head appeared at the top of the ladder, followed by the rest of her. She was wearing surfer shorts and a bikini top, and had a blue backpack on her shoulders.

"Hey, it looks really cool up here! This is sweet! It wasn't all done up like this when I was here the other night." She stood in the loft and surveyed the room. Then she crossed to the end of it, looked out at the sleeping porch, then turned back to take in the whole loft again. "Wow! I still can't believe your grandmother let you do this."

"Yeah, well, we *are* going to live out here now," said Neeve proudly, in spite of her feelings for Sloan. "It had to be nice."

"Huh. A great house, and all your cousins around." Sloan looked really envious for a minute, then seemed to catch herself and rearrange her features into their usual bored snottiness.

"Don't you have any cousins?" asked Neeve, suddenly feeling sorry for Sloan. Things were great for the Callahan cousins, and it just didn't seem that way for Sloan.

"Yeah . . . but . . . we don't really see them that much. And they're mostly boys." Sloan sounded wistful. "Actually, there's one girl my age, Melissa, and she's really cool. I mean, she was, the last time I saw her. But we don't get to see each other that much because our fathers don't really get along." Suddenly, she seemed to decide she'd said too much, and she clammed up.

Neeve knew she shouldn't judge Sloan's family too harshly. She'd thought her own family was the perfect normal family, and then after finding out her dad had been married before, and that he'd fought with Aunt Jean . . . Well, you just never knew. Families that seemed perfect usually weren't. But at least her family all loved one another. It was a good feeling. Safe, secure. Home.

Sloan seemed to be deciding whether or not to say something, and finally she did. "You guys are really lucky."

Neeve laughed. She couldn't believe Sloan would admit anything of the sort! "I was just thinking the same thing!" she said.

Sloan smiled.

Maybe she's not as bad as we think, thought Neeve briefly. *Maybe she's just always a jerk because she's jealous.*

But then Sloan's smile disappeared. "The reason I'm here is that, actually, my mother made me come." She paused.

"Okay . . . ," said Neeve, unsure of where this was going.

Sloan lifted her backpack off her shoulders and placed it at the foot of one of the beds. She unzipped it slowly, as if she was doing it against her will, and she pulled out a white envelope. "Here," she said, thrusting it awkwardly at Neeve.

"Oh," said Neeve tentatively. She wasn't sure whether to take it or not.

"Well, like I said, my mother found the makeup and . . . she got kind of mad at me. I was supposed to give it back to you immediately, but then it just disappeared." Sloan sounded nervous now. "I don't know how."

Neeve looked at Sloan and then reached over to the basket on top of her dresser. She pulled out her makeup bag and showed it to Sloan. "This reappeared the night of our cookout."

Sloan's eyes widened. "But how . . . ?"

"I don't know." Neeve shook her head solemnly. But she did, or she was beginning to think she did. That look Lark had shared with her that day at The Snack had popped back into her mind on Saturday, and she'd just had a feeling. She'd have to call Lark later to say thank you and see if she could get the full story. Neeve figured it must've been a little act of rebellion on Lark's part, taking the makeup and one-upping Sloan. Well, whatever; Neeve was just pleased to have her makeup back. And a new friend in Lark.

Sloan actually looked relieved, and surprisingly, she didn't press Neeve on the details. "Anyway, the photos. My mom said we didn't need them and that if you wanted them, you should have them. She was actually really furious at me about the whole thing. Here, think of them as a housewarming gift."

Neeve took the envelope and held it gingerly, as if it might burn her. She didn't open it. "Thanks."

Sloan smiled nervously and Neeve smiled back. They were each unsure of what to do or say next.

Neeve spontaneously unzipped her bag and rifled around

in it for a minute. Then she grabbed hold of something and presented it to Sloan with a flourish. "Here," she said.

Sloan looked down. It was the pot of red war paint from Kenya. She didn't reach for it.

"Go ahead," urged Neeve. "You can have it. It's just clay. I was only teasing about the blood. It makes a good lip stain because it doesn't come off."

Tentatively, Sloan took it and inspected it.

"You can tell people your friend from Africa got it for you," Neeve added generously. "But you have to tell them it's made from lions' blood, okay? That's part of the deal."

Sloan grinned and slipped the pot into her backpack. "Yeah. Okay."

Neeve placed the white envelope in the basket on top of her dresser. She'd look at the pictures some other time. Not now.

"Do you want to, uh, stay for a swim?" Neeve asked Sloan as she zipped up her backpack and looped it over her shoulders again. Neeve was feeling charitable toward Sloan for the moment. She knew it must've been hard for Sloan to admit she was wrong and to come back here. She also felt a tiny bit bad for Sloan that Lark, her supposed friend, had taken the Callahans' side. *But then again, who wouldn't?!* thought Neeve happily.

"Actually, Tucky's waiting in the car for me, so I have to go." Sloan hadn't changed. Neeve sighed in aggravation. She never would learn which way the wind was blowing when it came to Sloan.

"Okay. See you at clinic then. And thanks!"

"Sure."

And Sloan was gone.

Neeve glanced at the envelope again, then she had an idea. She grabbed it and crossed the loft to the sleeping porch door. Outside, she climbed the ladder to the lookout tower and then stood, looking out toward the direction of the Murray house.

But the trees had grown too tall in the past twenty years, and she couldn't make out the widow's walk. Oh well, she thought. It was just as well.

She tucked the photos into one of the rafters inside the tower's little turret. She would come back another day and look at them.

That night at their celebration dinner at Coolidge House, Gee toasted their success, and suggested they might want to tackle a few of the rooms in the big house next.

There were groans, especially from Phoebe and Hillary; they sure didn't want to start up another project again. But Neeve and Kate smiled at each other across the table. Now that things were comfortable between them, they'd consider tackling a project together again.

"Why, Gee? Are you lonely up there in the big house?" teased Neeve gently. She was privately worried that Gee was. And after all, the end of the summer was coming soon, and they'd all be gone. Only Gee and Sheila would stay.

"Maybe you need a boyfriend!" blurted Kate.

They all turned shocked eyes to Gee to see how she'd react. But she only laughed. "After Pops, I don't need any more men in my life. He was a full-time job, I'll tell you; more work than all nine kids put together." The girls giggled. Gee always joked about Pops, but they knew how great he'd been. "Anyhow, I love my independence. And I love being in my own home, on my own! What if I met someone and he wanted me to move to China or somewhere?"

"Then I'd come tutor you in Chinese!" cried Neeve happily.

"Oh my dear, the resources I have in all of you!" teased Gee. "I'd still hate to leave my home."

"Yeah, we know what you mean," agreed Neeve, her eyes shining with happiness. "Right, guys?" She stretched her fist out into the center of the table.

And while Gee looked on in amusement, the others all stacked their fists atop Neeve's, their rope bracelets appearing to join into one long rope.

"Cousins forever!" said Neeve solemnly, but a smile played at the corners of her mouth.

"Cousins forever!" the others echoed.

Here is a sneak peek of

The Callahan Cousins #3

Coming May 2006 from
Little, Brown and Company

CHAPTER ONE

Cool

Kate Callahan smiled before she'd even opened her eyes. She could sense the morning sunlight streaming in through the small, low windows of the Dorm, and she was thrilled that she and her cousins had finally accomplished their latest project: transforming the guesthouse at their grandmother Gee's summer estate into their very own home.

Kate loved crafts and needlework, artwork and cooking, but most of all, she loved creating little environments — basically, decorating, for lack of a better word. She enjoyed freshening up furniture, accessorizing a room, choosing new fabrics and colors: anything that could change the feel of a space from "blah" to "wow!" At home, her mother always invited her help on decorating projects around the house, and she allowed Kate to use her own room as a design lab. Because Kate was good at doing things herself, she'd sometimes change the color of her walls every other month, or rearrange her furniture over the weekend, with only a friend or two to help with the heavy stuff.

But working on the Dorm at Gee's had been totally different in a couple of ways. For one thing, she'd basically been able to start from scratch. There'd been no design when they started, and she'd had to come up with ideas for everything. That had been really exciting. But more important, she'd had to work and compromise with the three other cousins who were also staying at Gee's for the summer: Neeve, Phoebe, and Hillary, all of whom were twelve years old, like Kate. Compromise usually came easily to Kate; with two older brothers and a younger sister, she'd learned early how to negotiate and keep peace. She also had a slew of nice friends in Westchester, where she lived, and those friendships were peaceful and comfortable; there really wasn't much to fight about. But of course, she didn't live with any of them.

At Gee's house, however, Kate had fought bitterly with her cousin Neeve about everything from the wall color to how much time they were spending on the project. Back home, Kate had her own room, and her parents were very supportive of her interests, so she'd never really had to compromise when she was making decorating choices. She knew she had good taste, and she always had very specific ideas about what she wanted. But just last week she'd nearly lost her friendship with Neeve over paint color choices! In the end, they'd made up, and she'd actually ended up learning quite a lot about decorating from her worldly cousin: Neeve was all about putting in special touches that were more girly and fun, and also about being creative with unique materials and furniture that Kate normally would not have thought to use in decorating (like grass skirts, blackboard paint, and surfboards). The result was a true collaboration, and what Kate liked best about the Dorm was that it felt cool. It felt like a place teenagers would live; *cool* teenagers. And that's what she wanted to be.

Although she wouldn't turn thirteen until after the summer, Kate felt ready to reinvent herself — to renovate and redecorate her whole personality! And today was the day to start.

She scooted up out of her covers and reached for her diary in the bedside table beside her. She didn't really use it as a "Dear Diary" kind of book, but more as a list book — with lists of everything from lip gloss colors she liked to places she wanted to travel to, New Year's resolutions and stuff like that. The book was hardcover with pink flowered fabric glued around it. Pink flowers were kind of Kate's trademark; she used them whenever she could. Right now, in fact, a jug of pink roses stood blooming robustly on Kate's bedside table, and a needlepoint pillow of a pink daisy that she'd done rested on a side chair near the ladder that led to this sleeping loft.

Kate glanced across the room at the other three beds to make sure her cousins were still sleeping. It was only six-thirty, and they didn't have to be up for sailing clinic until seven, so she still had a few moments to herself. She uncapped her pink pen and turned to the next clean page in her diary.

COOL, she wrote across the top. And then she paused.

What do you have to do to be cool? she wondered. Neeve was certainly cool. She had lived all over the world, because her dad was in the U.S. Foreign Service and her mom was from Ireland. Neeve had lived in Ireland, Kenya, China, and now Singapore. She had friends in wild places, and lots of unusual makeup, and she could speak some really exotic languages. Plus she was a really good dresser; she made up zany outfits out of odds and ends that always managed to look effortlessly cool on her tiny, pixieish figure. And although her short black hair sprung up in cowlicks all over her head, her confidence and her little heart-shaped face with its bright blue Callahan eyes was so full of fun and mischief that an observer would wind up wishing she had black hair and cowlicks sticking up everywhere, too.

Hillary wasn't what Kate would call conventionally cool, but she wasn't uncool, either. She was really athletic and into what Kate considered ungirly stuff, like science and the environment. Also, she was from Colorado and she was forever camping or traveling somewhere with this or that varsity team she was on. She dressed really casually for the most part, in her Sweetie Sweats and other kinds of training gear, and her strawberry-blond curls always seemed to be wet from an after-workout shower or from swimming. Although Hillary wasn't what Kate aspired to be like, she was independent and not a follower at all; she had friends and was happy, and didn't just go with the flow.

And then there was Phoebe. She was probably the least cool, in the true sense of the word, but she was also the least likely to care if people thought she was cool or not. She was from Florida, and she was really, really, really super smart and bookish. She knew a lot about everything. She had an older sister and a younger sister, and a tight group of equally bookish friends back home, who were all on the yearbook committee and the newspaper staff at school together. They thought it was fun to stay up late studying and quizzing each other for school. Phoebe was beautiful, but she didn't realize it or do anything with it, and somehow that made her less beautiful. Because even though she was tall and willowy, with white-blond hair that she'd inherited from her gorgeous Swedish mother, she dressed like a hippie (albeit a neat one), and did nothing to enhance her amazing looks. She actually kind of hid them, with glasses, and ugly buns in her hair and stuff. (The cousins had gotten a glimpse of how gorgeous Phoebe could be when they'd given her a makeover recently; everyone had been awed by the results). *Gosh,* thought Kate wistfully, *if I could look the way Phoebe does with makeup, that would really be cool.*

Kate herself was not very tall. She wasn't very thin, either, nor was she muscular and lean like Hillary. She had long brown hair that her mother called "chestnut" and Kate called "dog poop brown," and she didn't tan evenly like Phoebe or look great in weird clothes like Neeve. She was preppy and girly, and she favored the color pink. The sun burned her, and her blue eyes were sensitive to bright light, and she preferred quiet indoor activities to anything that required physical strength, daring, or bravery of any sort. And at the moment, she was feeling very disappointed in herself. It was time for a change.

She sighed quietly. Cool. Cool. What did she need to do? Neeve rolled over and murmured in her sleep two beds away, and Kate leaned forward to peek at her.

Maybe a haircut? Kate thought, studying Neeve for outward signs of coolness. *Or a new wardrobe? Maybe I should learn to speak some exotic language? Or . . .* She glanced over at Hillary . . . *get really good at a sport? Or maybe I should become an expert on something cool, like . . . um . . .* She stared absentmindedly at Phoebe as she racked her brain for ideas.

Suddenly Phoebe cracked one eye open and stared back at Kate.

"What?" she huffed. Phoebe was not a morning person.

Kate was startled. "Nothing. Um . . ."

"Why are you sitting there writing in your diary about me like you're Harriet the Spy or someone?" demanded Phoebe.

"Oh, Bee . . . I'm not writing about you, you silly goose!" Kate smiled affectionately at her cousin. "I'm just making a list. A To Do list." *Yes. That was what it was, after all,* thought Kate.

"Well stare elsewhere while you do it!" Phoebe rolled over and pulled her duvet up over her head to block out the morning light. She'd be sound asleep again in thirty seconds and probably never remember that this conversation had taken place.

Meanwhile, Kate turned back to her diary and began to scribble furiously. Now that her brain was fully awake, all sorts of ideas were coming to her and she had goose bumps of excitement at the possibilities for change. *What is the recipe for a successful transformation to coolness? Could it be as easy as a makeover? A diet? A new name? A new best friend? Or would it take a combination of all of the above, plus a little extra something?* wondered Kate.

Inspiration struck as she wrote, and Kate grinned and flipped back to the inside cover of the book where she'd written her name. KATE CALLAHAN, it said, in pretty, loopy script. Kate paused for a moment and then crossed it out, artfully turning the scribble into a colored-in pink heart. Then, underneath it, she wrote in a new and unfamiliar but . . . cool, yes, definitely *cool* scratchy print: *Cate Callahan.* Cool girl, she added silently. Yes. Definitely.

Liz Carey is a former children's book editor. She lives in New York City with her husband and two young sons, and she has twenty-five first cousins of her own.